"You liked that kiss as much as I did. Admit it."

"I will not admit anything," Gianna insisted. "Besides, it was all for show."

"But what if it wasn't?" Gage asked.

"I don't deal in what-ifs, Gage."

"I'm just saying, what if that kiss wasn't a fluke? What if it's the best kiss either one of us ever had? What if we try it again, just to be sure?"

"You want to kiss me again? Right here and now? Without an audience? No, thanks."

"Nervous?"

"Gage, be serious. Don't even go there."

"You don't even know how tempting you are."

"Cut it out. I'm going to bed."

"I don't suppose that's an invitation?"

* * *

The Fake Engagement Favor by Charlene Sands is part of The Texas Tremaines series.

Dear Reader,

Hello and welcome back to the Tremaine family! This time around you'll meet country music superstar Gage Tremaine, brother of Lily and Cade. Gage is in for the ride of his life when he enters into a fake-engagement scheme to repair his bad-boy image. He's being considered for a greatly coveted starring role in a family-based movie.

The only one Gage trusts with this deception is family friend Gianna Marino. She's the perfect choice for his pretend fiancée—a university professor, a woman with brains and a great reputation in the community. He's known Gianna for years and their mothers are best friends. Becoming engaged—in name only—to the professor would help elevate him from his fall from grace and secure his future.

The fun begins when Gage puts a ring on Gianna's finger. She's no pushover—Gage has met his match in the girl he always tormented as a kid. But their phony embraces and staged smoldering kisses soon prove that opposites really do attract. Oh boy, do they attract!

When I set out to write this story, I knew Gage would be cocky but kind, flamboyant but sincere, and then I found brilliant Gianna, the family friend, the one who'd never refuse the Tremaines a favor. I knew there was more to her than her intelligence. She was an equal match for the superstar in all ways and *The Fake Engagement Favor* was born!

Happy reading, all, and let me know how you like the story!

Sincerely,

Charlene

CHARLENE SANDS

———

THE FAKE ENGAGEMENT FAVOR

HARLEQUIN

DESIRE

DESIRE™

Recycling programs for this product may not exist in your area.

ISBN-13: 978-1-335-73513-3

The Fake Engagement Favor

Copyright © 2021 by Charlene Swink

This edition published by arrangement with Harlequin Books S.A.

For questions and comments about the quality of this book, please contact us at CustomerService@Harlequin.com.

Harlequin Enterprises ULC
22 Adelaide St. West, 40th Floor
Toronto, Ontario M5H 4E3, Canada
www.Harlequin.com

Printed in U.S.A.

Charlene Sands is a *USA TODAY* bestselling author of contemporary romance and stories set in the American West. She's been honored with the National Readers' Choice Award, the CataRomance Reviewers' Choice Award and is a double recipient of the Booksellers' Best Award. Her 2014 Harlequin Desire title was named the Best Desire of the Year.

Charlene knows a little something about romance—she married her high school sweetheart! And her perfect day includes reading, drinking mocha cappuccinos, watching Hallmark movies and riding bikes with her hubby. She has two adult children and four sweet young princesses, who make her smile every day. Visit her at charlenesands.com to keep up with her new releases and fun contests. Find her on Facebook, Twitter and Instagram, too: Facebook.com/charlenesandsbooks and Twitter.com/charlenesands.

Books by Charlene Sands

Harlequin Desire

The Texas Tremaines

Craving a Real Texan
The Fake Engagement Favor

The Slades of Sunset Ranch

Sunset Surrender
Sunset Seduction
The Secret Heir of Sunset Ranch
Redeeming the CEO Cowboy

Visit her Author Profile page at Harlequin.com, or charlenesands.com, for more titles.

You can also find Charlene Sands on Facebook, along with other Harlequin Desire authors, at Facebook.com/HarlequinDesireAuthors.

Dedicated to my sweet daughter,
Nikki, with all my love.

You deserve all good and wonderful things in life!

Happy Birthday!

One

"Are we really going to do this?" Gianna asked handsome, cocky Gage Tremaine. She sat on a patio chair facing the gorgeously groomed Tremaine estate, hardly believing she'd agreed to being Gage's newfound love. His pretend fiancée, for heaven's sake, until the country music superstar got his life back on track.

"Do you have a boyfriend or someone who'd object to this?"

"Just…uh, no. Not at the moment," she said quietly.

"Then I think we're doing it," he drawled in the Texas twang that his fans adored. "I hate to admit this, but you're the perfect choice. You're out of the public eye and have a very honorable profession. You're smart and upstanding and a good family friend. It makes sense, Gianna."

She was all those things, yet hearing Gage say it made it all seem so…uninspiring.

"But I'm hardly your type." She wasn't. Not by a long shot. She wasn't stylish or trendy. She wore her hair in a messy bun at the top of her head most times and could barely see a thing without her eyeglasses.

"Are you suggesting you're too darn intelligent for me, Professor Marino?"

Good God. He would go there. At times, she wasn't even sure she liked Gage all that much. He was always teasing her, about her brains, about her looks. She'd grown up around the Tremaines, and she wasn't gonna lie, Gage had been like a thorn in her side. But then he'd smile and tell her he didn't mean it, and she'd forgive him.

"You know I am."

He grinned. "True."

His incredible blue eyes darkened and then a serious expression stole over his face. "I know this is a lot to ask. But I'm in a bind and Regan Fitzgerald, my manager, came up with this little scheme to make nice with the press. I don't like it, either, but I have to restore my image. I've been at this a long time, and I'm no saint, but I'm also not as bad as people make me out to be. My record sales are down some."

"And you need to land that film role in *Sunday in Montana*."

"Bad boys don't get the lead in a family movie."

"I get it. But—but there must be dozens of girls

out there who'd like to play house with you, even if it is pretend."

"I wouldn't *trust* anyone but you," he said, his eyes clear, revealing the truth. "If word got out, this could ruin me."

"Really?" He had that much faith in her? Well, he should. She would never betray a Tremaine. They were her second family, going back decades. Her mother and Rose Tremaine, Gage's mom, had been like sisters. Rose had been a godsend when her mama got sick. She'd helped pay the medical bills a young local Fairmont University professor couldn't afford.

Rose had held her hand when her mama passed on, their quiet sobs binding them ever closer.

"Yeah, according to Regan, if it slipped that I hired someone to be my fake fiancée, after all the other scandals I've had this past year, I'd stand to lose my reputation for good."

"You have had quite a few," she said tactfully. Three scandals, to be exact, and each time, Gage had a valid excuse or reason for what transpired. He made headlines, and often the media printed lies about the eligible bachelor with the deep, sexy voice that drove women wild. Even she had to admit that Gage had immense talent. And she wasn't even a fan of country music. "You almost lost your life over the last one."

Gage put his hand up to his neck, carefully touching the wound that was still visible from the barroom brawl where a broken bottle slashed his throat. "Don't remind me. I learned my lesson on that one."

"Don't try to rescue a damsel in distress?"

"Don't butt in when a girl is arguing with her boyfriend. But, in my own defense, what I saw at the bar was a drunken cowboy manhandling a woman against her wishes."

The way Gage told it, once the police arrived, he was bleeding at the throat from a broken bottle, his band members were all banged up and the bar was a total mess. To top it off, the girl had stuck up for her abusive boyfriend instead of siding with Gage. He wound up getting blamed for starting the fight and had paid for all the damages. His photo was splashed across the covers of all the tabloids, taking down his reputation one more notch.

The other two scandals weren't violent yet had dragged his name through the mud. Cheating on his girlfriend—and pushing a news reporter to the ground when asked about it—wasn't a way to win friends and gain influence. Gage claimed his innocence on both, but it didn't matter. The paparazzi ate it all up.

Rose walked outside carrying a tray of Texas sun tea and cookies. Gianna's mind flashed to another time, a happier time. Mom and Rose having their sun tea on this very deck.

A knot formed in her stomach. It was still so new to her, losing her mother. The pain never went away. She couldn't stop thinking about her.

"Have some iced tea, Gianna. Gage, will you pour it?" She set the tray down on a side table.

"Sure, Mom." He rose and looked up from the tray. "There's only two glasses here."

"Yes, I'm going to let you two talk some more. I came out here to tell you, Gianna, that there's no pressure if you refuse Gage's request." Rose put a hand on her arm and squeezed. "I know it's a lot to ask of you, sweetheart."

"Look, when we travel, I promise we'll always get a suite with two rooms. And you'll have plenty of time to do your research," Gage said.

"And it would only be for a month, right?"

"Six or seven weeks," he said. "Long enough for me to make some scheduled appearances and nail down that role."

That would be most of the summer. "What happens after that?"

"Well, we haven't quite figured that out yet. But once summer is over, you'd have to go back to teaching, right?" he asked.

She nodded.

"And hopefully, our story would fade into the background if there are no more rumors or scandals. We could have a quiet breakup sometime in the future."

"The future? As in how long?"

Gage shrugged. "Not sure. Does it matter?"

Rose shot her son a hard look. "Of course it matters. Gianna can't put her life on hold indefinitely."

His assumption that she had no life, or *love life*, outside of teaching rattled her. She dated once in a while. Okay, but only when her friend Brooke set her up on blind dates. She did have a keen affection for Timothy Bellamy, a history professor at the university. But so far, all they'd had were a few coffee dates. No sparks yet, but she was mourning her mother and focused on her career—she wasn't exactly in the market for sparks.

"Sorry, right." He scrubbed at his stubbled jaw.

Rose looked her in the eye and smiled sweetly. "Remember, if you decide you can't do this, everyone will understand. You're always going to be a part of this family."

"Thanks, Rose. That means a lot."

Rose kissed her cheek and left the patio.

She turned to Gage. "Your mom always makes me feel so welcome."

"She loves you, Gianna."

"She misses Mom almost as much as I do."

"Yeah, your mother was pretty awesome."

"She was a fan of yours, too, even before your fame." Though, for the life of her, Gianna couldn't understand why. She released a deep sigh. "I still can't believe she's gone."

Gage nodded. He was quiet for a while, staring out to the landscape before him. He wasn't always cocky and smug. Sometimes he was nice, and she couldn't imagine turning down his request. She owed the Tremaine family her loyalty, and this would be one way to repay their kindness. Her heart hurt every day, and maybe helping Gage would take her mind off her grief for a little bit.

"I'm a terrible liar," she blurted. "I'm in a committed relationship with the truth."

Gage blinked, his head jerking back, and he took a

few moments to process her blunt declaration. "Most of what we say will be the truth. We're childhood friends, and we became reacquainted this summer. And we realized our feelings for each other…"

"After you were injured in that brawl?"

"That works. You're not such a bad liar after all."

"I'm a problem solver, Gage. Not a liar. We need to puzzle this out before the public sees us together."

"So, then, you're sure?"

She nodded, totally unsure, but she wasn't going to refuse to help a Tremaine. Even if it meant going against all her well-honed instincts. "When do we get engaged?"

Gage grinned, his teeth flashing in a bright smile. He was good-looking to a fault, and talented, a golden boy who somehow had to pretend to be in love with her.

It would put his acting chops to the test. He could probably pull it off.

But could she?

"You know the last person who lived in this guesthouse ended up falling in love with my brother Cade," Gage's sister, Lily, told Gianna.

Gianna flopped onto the sofa next to Lily, grabbed a pillow and tucked it under her arms. Over the years she'd stayed on the property many times, sometimes at the main house, sometimes here in this cottage guesthouse. She enjoyed the privacy afforded her here, where she could pull her thoughts together without interference. "I've met Harper. She's perfectly suited for Cade. And vice versa."

"I know. I'm happy I had a hand in getting them together. Though not purposely. But it all worked out. Who knows what will happen between you and Gage?" Lily grinned at her, and Gianna's mouth dropped open.

"Lily, whatever you're thinking, don't. Nothing like that's going to happen between me and Gage. He's…he's…not my type."

"You have a type?"

"No. Yes. I suppose I do. Someone who's into fine art, history and philosophy."

"Ah, so you mean, not someone who sings for his supper and has women dropping at his feet?"

Gianna rolled her eyes. "I'm not impressed by those things."

Lily didn't appear convinced. "I'm just saying, Gage can be charming. He may just surprise you."

"I'm fully prepared to deal with Gage. When the time comes." She could go head to head with him in mental battles all day long. It was the other part of the deal that worried her. She'd always been true to herself and honest in her feelings. So this pretense didn't come naturally to her. Like she'd told Gage, she was committed to telling the truth. And she'd meant it.

"That time may be coming sooner than you think. We have one week before the family's big Fourth of July celebration. That's where Gage plans to announce your engagement."

This was all becoming very real. In a week's time,

their little charade would begin, and a part of her welcomed the distraction. It would keep her grief at bay, but a larger part of her felt uncertain and wary. Gianna rose from the sofa and walked over to the beveled glass window, catching her reflection through the pane. She saw a grieving woman with pale olive skin, plain clothes and thick-rimmed glasses. Her shoulders drooped, and she turned to Lily. "Do you think anyone's going to believe that Gage and I are in love?"

"Gage will convince them."

But Gianna needed more than that. She needed to feel confident that she could pull this off. "Lily? I think I need your help."

"With?"

"You're an interior designer and quite talented at what you do. But have you ever worked with exteriors?"

"Yes, sometimes. I've reworked and renovated outdoor patios and verandas and such. In fact, I just finished revamping a pool and lounge exterior for the Goldens' estate down the road."

"I meant, human exteriors?"

Lily caught her meaning and gave her a look. "You want a makeover?"

"No, I don't *want* a makeover, but I think I need one. It's not going to be easy pretending, especially since I don't fit into Gage's world. At all. But if I looked the part, it might make it easier for me."

Lily gave her an assessing once-over. Gianna removed her eyeglasses and immediately began to squint.

"Have you ever tried contacts?"

"Yes, but they irritate my eyes."

"Actually, your face is well suited for glasses. You don't need contacts. And honestly, you're quite lovely, Gianna. You just need to highlight your best features. Just a little. And maybe have a wardrobe renovation." Lily smiled.

"So, you'll do it?"

"Of course. It's not going to be a drastic change, but you'd be surprised what a little makeup and a new hairstyle can do for a woman. Here, let me show you what I mean with your wardrobe."

She followed Lily to the foyer mirror.

"Some things need to be tweaked," Lily said. "Like this boxy white blouse you're wearing. It's long and gives you no shape at all. But watch this," Lily said, rolling up the sleeves above her elbows and unbuttoning the bottom three buttons of the blouse. Next, she took the tails of the blouse, pulled them taut and tied a knot right at her waistline. "There. Take a look at the difference. From baggy to stylish, with just a little ingenuity."

Gianna studied herself in the mirror. She still had a long way to go, but in just under a minute, Lily had really made a big difference.

"Tomorrow we'll go to the salon, give that thick hair of yours some pretty highlights and a fresh cut. And then we'll go shopping."

"Thanks, Lily."

"You're welcome. But you know, Gage doesn't expect you to do all this."

"I'm not doing it for him, Lil. I kinda need to do this for myself."

"I get it. You're such a good friend, Gianna." Lily squeezed her tight, and the affection brought warmth to her heart.

If she was going to play the part, it only made sense to go all in.

Gianna never did anything halfway.

Gage stood at the guesthouse door, ready to knock. He wasn't ready for this date, a trip to the town ice cream shop. He'd thought he'd have at least a few more days before the charade would begin. In his opinion it wasn't necessary, but his manager, Regan, had other ideas. *You need to be seen in public a few times before you actually get engaged. It'll make it look more realistic.*

He didn't agree, but Regan knew how to get him out of a bind—she was an expert at it—and he'd finally learned to listen to her.

So now, here he was trapped into going on a first date with Gianna. He should be glad he'd convinced her while on the phone. She was doing him a big favor. But she didn't like this idea any more than he did, so he wouldn't feel guilty about it. Neither of them wanted to do this. And in typical Gianna form, she'd overanalyzed the situation, making her arguments why they shouldn't be going out until the big engagement announcement. It would have less impact on the press. It was too soon. Neither of them was ready.

Gianna wasn't wrong about any of these things, but Regan had a point. It had to look like their relationship was evolving naturally.

He knocked on the door, trying to adjust his frown into some semblance of a smile. He waited almost a minute, then knocked again.

Finally, the door opened and Gianna appeared.

At least he thought it was Gianna. Well, damn. It was her, all right. For a second, his throat closed up. What the hell? Her hair was cut to just past her shoulders, glossed to a deep chestnut brown and parted on the side. Thin-rimmed glasses kept hair from falling onto her cheeks and amplified her gorgeous light green eyes through the lenses. She wore a halter-top denim dress that exposed a hint of eye-popping cleavage. Gianna had cleavage? She'd always worn superbaggy clothes that hid her female shape.

There was a blush to her complexion, and he wasn't sure if it was due to his immediate reaction to her. The slight rosy color blended with her smooth olive skin. He scanned her up and down, catching the strappy sandals encasing her feet, her toenails painted a pale pink.

"You're staring," she said.

He was. He couldn't take his eyes off her, and that wasn't good. He didn't like the jolts of electricity shooting through his system. He didn't like the attraction that immediately caused his breath to catch. Gianna was…stunning.

He hadn't signed up for this. He hadn't reacted this way to a woman in years; the instant magnetism shifted his perspective into something he didn't recognize. Gianna was forbidden fruit, and he'd have to remember that. She was like family, a girl he'd known for years and the daughter of his mother's best friend. To top it off, she was in mourning and very vulnerable right now.

"What did you do to yourself?" It was his knee-jerk response to her hot appearance. Emphasis on *jerk*. It pissed him off that she'd made this transformation, giving him a bit of a shock and throwing him off balance.

Her chin went up. "Nothing," she said sharply.

"Brainiac, you've done something."

"Brickhead, I thought you were taking me for ice cream?"

His mouth twitched, but he held back a smile. Using their childhood nicknames for each other oddly put him at ease. When they were kids, he'd played with her unless there'd been something better to do. Admittedly, he'd sorta tormented her, but Gianna never cowered. She'd held her ground and dished out equal justice. He'd always admired that about her. She didn't back down. Nope, she was too quick, too clever to let him get the best of her. "I am. Ready to go?"

Taking her to the best ice cream shop in Juliet, Triple Scoop, was the only way he could coax her into going out tonight. If memory served, she could devour a Triple Decker without batting an eyelash.

She nodded. "Let's get this over with."

He couldn't agree more, but somehow hearing her say it stung.

In the driveway, he opened the passenger side door for her and caught a glimpse of her tanned legs as she flounced into the seat. She caught him looking, and he pretended not to notice. He climbed in, started the engine of his midnight-blue Aston Martin and sped off.

Halfway to town, Gage glanced over at Gianna. "I'm not complaining, but why'd you do it?"

She turned her face away to stare out the window. "Seems like you are complaining."

"Are you gonna answer my question?"

She pushed air out of her lungs. The sigh was dramatic and real. "It only makes sense, Gage. I weighed the options and came to the conclusion that if we're to have people believe we're together, I need to look the part. Lily gave me some help."

"Lily did a good job."

"Is that a backhanded compliment?"

His lips twitched again. She'd made it clear—she hadn't dressed to impress, or at least to impress *him*. It was a calculated move on her part to ensure their little scheme worked. Gianna wasn't the type to fish for compliments, but he owed her this one. "You look very pretty, Gianna."

It was the understatement of the year.

"Thank you," she replied.

Once in town, he parked the car two blocks from the ice cream shop, and Gianna glanced at him curiously. "Why are we parking here?"

"A little walk will do us good."

"Let me guess, Regan's idea? So more people will see us together?"

He didn't give her the satisfaction of an answer, because she was right and he hated to admit it. "Usually the townsfolk don't pester me too much, but, just a warning, that all might change when I'm spotted with you on my arm."

He got out of the car, opened the car door for her and offered his hand.

She slipped her hand in his, and the delicate softness of her skin pummeled through him as he helped her step out. He closed the door and set the car alarm. It beeped and off they went, strolling down the street hand in hand.

A bright sunset was making its descent, the summer air heavy and thick. Beads of sweat circled his neck and made his jeans stick to his legs. Gianna seemed unaffected by the heat. She walked along the street, her chin up, her cool demeanor unmarred. A few women came out of a lingerie store and stopped to gape. Quickly, they took out their phones and snapped pictures of Gage and Gianna. One lady approached and asked for a selfie.

"Sure, let's get Gianna in on this, too," he told her.

The woman didn't hesitate. "Okay."

She snapped a picture of the three of them and then thanked them, giving Gianna a puzzled look. Her wheels must've been turning as she wondered who his date was. Soon, hopefully, everyone would know. Gage took Gianna's hand again and ventured on.

He was stopped two more times by fans who

wanted photos before they entered the crowded ice cream shop. "No doubt those photos will be all over the internet in less than an hour," Gianna whispered. "I guess Regan knows what she's talking about."

"Yep, she usually does."

She'd been his manager for going on nine years now. She hadn't steered him wrong on any of the decisions they'd made. Any trouble he'd been involved in wasn't a result of bad managing. He'd gotten into that trouble all on his own, but lucky for him, Regan knew how to prevent his image from tanking. He just had to keep his nose clean for the next six weeks or so and he could move on with his life.

Gianna sat across the round café table from Gage, bringing her tongue across the top layer of her Triple Decker, feeling self-conscious as at least a dozen pairs of eyes darted glances her way. Gage had already signed four autographs for giddy girls who deemed themselves lucky to have had an ice cream craving at the same time he did. They lingered, watching his every move, and not until he'd finally given them a wave and a "See ya" did they dash back to their own table, cell phones in hand, typing as fast as their thumbs would allow.

"Geesh, is it always like this?" Gianna asked.

"This is nothing," Gage said. "Sometimes I have to run for my life."

"You're joking, right?"

He shook his handsome head, his eyes twinkling.

"The forty-year-olds are worse than these kids. They want a piece of me I'm not willin' to give."

"Like what?" She took another lick of her cone. The Triple Decker consisted of three scoops of your favorite flavors along with toppings for each layer. She was demolishing rocky road with raspberry topping at the moment, with a scoop of French vanilla topped with chocolate sprinkles and a scoop of mocha fudge, swimming in nuts, just waiting for her. Ice cream was the guiltiest guilty pleasures and her weak spot.

"They try to rip off my clothes. And touch places they have no business touching."

"Really, they do that?" She was appalled. Even though celebrities expected to be adored by their fans, and wanted to be, there were limits. No one had a right to abuse those boundaries.

"Concerts are the worst. The venues provide security teams, but every once in a while someone gets by them. It's why I need a bodyguard sometimes."

"So where is he now?"

"He gets time off when I'm home in Juliet. Like I said, the townsfolk aren't out for my blood. They let me live my life, pretty much."

"Glad to hear that."

"That's all gonna change on the Fourth. Regan's got all the local news reporters coming. That's when things will heat up." His gaze slid down to her mouth as she licked her cone. "You're sure enjoying that."

The look in his eyes made her edgy. "My favorite."

"I remember."

"You're a party poop for not getting the Triple."

Unfazed, he licked at his all-chocolate cone, one scoop. No toppings. "Sometimes more is not better."

She wound her tongue around the last of her rocky road. "Oh, but when it's better, it's way better."

"Hold on a sec," he said, reaching into his pocket. "Let's get a picture of this. Our first date."

"Probably smart to document it."

"Yeah," he said, nodding. "That's what I was going for."

His head came close to hers, enough so that she could smell his scent—something expensive, oozing with masculinity. "Smile," he told her.

She did, and he snapped the photo.

"That's perfect," he said, glancing at the picture, grinning like a fool.

"Let me see it."

He handed her the phone. She glimpsed her image and gasped. "You!"

In the photo, Gianna was smiling, but her mouth was smudged all over with raspberry sauce. She looked like a ten-year-old kid, and right now, she felt like one, too. She grabbed a napkin, wiped her mouth, then crumpled it up and tossed it at him. "You never change."

He caught the napkin on a chuckle. "That's what you get for calling me, of all people, a party poop."

"So you're saying *I* started it?"

"If the shoe fits, Cinderella."

She felt like Cinderella, playing dress-up with the handsome prince. But unlike Cinderella, she'd be happy when the ball ended, so she could go back to being her own pumpkin self again.

She deleted the picture, then caught a few photos of him with his band. Some were taken while he was onstage, lights beaming down, his hat shadowing his face and beads of sweat dripping down. She imagined his fans standing up, singing along with him, knowing the words to all his songs.

This was what he was trying to hang on to. This was what he was trying to protect. He wasn't just a newbie country singer with a few hits. He was a brand all his own and carried the weight of countless behind-the-scenes crew members on his shoulders, as well as many other vendors and producers and musicians.

She gave him back his phone, sobered now. "It's not about the money, is it, Gage? That's not why we're doing this."

He didn't pretend not to know what she was talking about. "It never was."

He was rich in his own right. His family was one of the wealthiest in all of Texas. But she couldn't imagine Gage working in an office, going over ledgers and spreadsheets. Gage had a freer spirit than that. He was talented and loved what he did for a living. He wanted to be the one to decide when his career ended, not the other way around. In a sense, he was fighting for that right. To decide his own future. And as silly as having a fake fiancée seemed, she understood why he was invested in this ruse.

"I know," she said.

"Gianna, sometimes you get me better than anyone else."

"Is that why you always picked on me?"

He shrugged, thinking on it. "You were the one person I couldn't fool. Sorta pissed me off, if I'm being honest."

He infuriated her at times, but she never let him see it. "Now we're grown-ups and we can forget playing those silly gotcha games. We have a goal in mind and we should stick to it, Gage."

"Where's the fun in that?"

"Nothing about this is fun for me."

His smile waned, and the joy in his expression disappeared.

She wouldn't rub it in too much, but she was doing him a big favor. And she wanted it to go smoothly, without any bumps in the road. Putting up with the insufferable Gage Tremaine for the summer wasn't her idea of a good time.

They finished their cones, and Gage offered his hand when it was time to leave. He held on firmly and then kissed her cheek, a subtle little peck, but one that told all the roving eyes in the ice cream shop that she was his and vice versa.

And that peck came as a complete surprise. Her face tingled where his lips had touched her skin. That subtle touch and the way he'd looked at her when she'd opened the guesthouse door worried her. Because she'd felt something spark and sizzle inside her. For a moment.

Gianna held a secret close to her heart, one that

ensured she wouldn't fall for Gage. It was something she'd never told another soul. Something that made her avoid men like Gage Tremaine. All she would ever have with Gage was a fake engagement. Period.

There was no doubt Gage was an appealing man. But she didn't want to notice. She didn't want to be charmed. She supposed that at some point Gage would actually have to kiss her in front of an audience.

And she dreaded it.

Two

Gianna stood facing Juliet Jewelry on Main Street, Gage by her side. It'd been two days since their date at the ice cream shop, and social media had been all abuzz with news of their romance. Now they were making a pit stop at the jewelry store before their dinner date. "I still don't think we need to do this," she said, feeling grossly uncomfortable. She didn't know why Gage insisted on buying her a ring. "I can wear my mother's ring, Gage. It's a pretty engagement band."

Gage shook his head. "We've been over this already. I need to buy you a ring to make things look official. If this were real, you'd have a rock on your left hand that everyone would notice."

He looked at her hand. "Besides, you've worn that

ring on your right hand since your mama passed," he said softly. "It wouldn't be right to use it that way."

She sensed he was being considerate so she couldn't fault him. He was adamant about getting her a ring, and this was one argument she wasn't going to win. "Okay, fine. But I don't want anything flashy."

"I wouldn't think you'd do flashy. Whatever size and shape you want is what you'll have, Gianna." Gage took her hand. "Ready to do this?"

She nodded. "Yes. Let's go pick out a ring."

Gage had made special arrangements with the shop owner for a private appointment, and they were greeted immediately by a man named Jeffrey Danes as they entered the store. Marble floors and rich stone walls spoke of class and wealth. The shop wasn't large, but the three long cases set in a horseshoe shape were cleaned to a brilliant shine and displayed all manner of jewels. Overhead, a spectacular sparkling chandelier hung in the center of the room.

"Jeffrey, I'd like to introduce you to my girlfriend, Professor Gianna Marino."

The man took her hand without giving it a shake. "Pleasure to meet you. I hope we can find the perfect ring for you. And congratulations on your upcoming engagement."

Heat rushed up her neck. She hated lying. "Thank you very much."

"We haven't announced our engagement yet," Gage said. "And we'd appreciate your discretion until we make the announcement."

"Always," Jeffrey assured them. "I've been doing

business with your family for years. You can trust me. Now, let me show you our best-quality rings." He gestured to the case at the back of the shop. Already, Gianna's hackles were raised. She didn't want to wear an expensive ring. She didn't want Gage to spend a fortune for a ring she was only going to return to him. It wasn't necessary. None of this was.

"Have a seat, please."

They both sat on plush chairs as the man pulled out a black velvet drawer and set it on top of the jewel case, giving Gage a big smile. Gianna nearly choked seeing the size of the diamonds.

"You can have any one you want, sweetheart," Gage said, dead serious.

"Do any of these lovely rings interest you?" Jeffrey asked. "They are of the finest quality and, as you can see, very unique in style."

Was Gage crazy? Or was he putting on a good show? No way was she going to pick out a ring that cost more than his sports car. She shook that notion off and pretended interest in the six rings shown to her, taking a bit of time, trying to play the part, but then shook her head. "They are a bit ornate for my taste. Do you have something simpler? And smaller?"

Gage's mouth twitched. He was amused by her discomfort.

Jeffrey blinked, hiding his true emotions. He wasn't going to make a killing on a ring today. "Of course. I have an entire array of rings to show you. Or, if you prefer, you can pick out a setting and we can find you the perfect diamond."

"Oh, no. That's not necessary. I'm sure I can find one I like." Gianna rose from her seat and wandered the shop, only to stop at a case up at the front of the store. "May I see these?" she asked, pointing to group of solitaire rings.

Jeffrey rushed right over. "Oh, those aren't—"

Gage was right behind him. "Aren't what?"

"They're, uh, fine and all. We only carry the best, but are you sure?" He looked at Gianna.

"I'd like to see the marquise, please." She pointed to a ring any woman wouldn't mind wearing—if they weren't getting engaged to a superstar. She didn't want to give Jeffrey a stroke, but she wasn't going to pick anything worth over a few thousand dollars.

"It's a solitaire, platinum band, but I'm afraid it's only one carat." He slid the door open and took out the ring. "Here you go," he said, setting the ring down on a square of black velvet, trying not to appear annoyed. Jeffrey probably hadn't run into too many women who were given carte blanche and then opted for such a small, plain ring. "Try it on if you'd like."

"Is that the one you like the most, Gianna?" Gage asked.

She put the ring on her left ring finger. "It's simple and just the right size for me. Yes, I'd love this one."

Gage looked at Jeffrey. "I think the lady has found her ring."

"Yes, yes. Good choice," he told Gianna as he tried to show some enthusiasm.

"Gianna, why don't you look around a bit while I settle up with Jeffrey?" Gage kissed her cheek for good measure, and she sucked in a breath at the sensation of his lips on her skin yet again. She walked out of the store, needing to clear her head. She'd just picked out a ring for her fake engagement—just one lie of many more to come.

So it hadn't been a fluke the other day. Gianna had dressed for their second date in a fitted cream lace dress that highlighted her tiny waist and dipped into delicious cleavage at the neckline. Her meadow-green eyes dazzled from behind her glasses, and the overhead lights in the Rhinestone Room reflected on her hair. Again, she looked amazing. His soon-to-be fiancée. She'd given poor Jeffrey at the jewelry store a migraine for sure by picking out the least expensive ring in his shop. Practical, analytical and ever-cautious Gianna didn't want to stick him with a hefty price tag. Little did she know that the ring was hers. He wouldn't take it back under any circumstances. It was a small price to pay for her help.

As the maître d' led them to a table at the back of the restaurant, heads turned, but this time it was Gianna who captured the attention. Not him. Not only did she look pretty, but she was now a bit of a curiosity. Compounding the social media buzz, local papers and online news outlets had already picked up on Gage Tremaine's latest love interest, and while they didn't know who she was, the photos at the ice cream shop spoke volumes.

Once seated, Gage ordered red wine as soft music played throughout the restaurant. Cellphones popped out of hiding from the other patrons, and they seemed to snap endless photos of the two of them. Gage had learned not to engage with his audience, not to look them in the eye. He'd learned to keep his focus on his dinner dates and enjoy himself, despite having his every move scrutinized. He'd always chosen a back table for that very reason. It made it harder for people to be discreet with their observations and photo trigger fingers. Though it went against his motives, he wanted to have a few private moments with Gianna.

"Have you been here before?" he asked Gianna.

"Yes, several times."

"With a date?" he blurted. Damn, he hadn't intended to sound incredulous.

"Would that surprise you?"

"No. But, uh, never mind." The Rhinestone Room was exclusive, and it wasn't a place you took a woman unless you were serious about her. Not only was the food excellent and the service impeccable, but it made a statement. It said, *you're special*. And it had been Regan's idea to bring Gianna here to send the right message.

"If you must know, I was honored with an award here just last year."

He lifted his brows. He wasn't surprised, but rather, impressed. "What was it for?"

"I received the Fairmont Faculty Award for Excellence in Teaching. We had a special dinner here."

"Congratulations. I bet your mom was proud."

Gage shouldn't have brought up her mother, but

it was too late. Fortunately, Gianna didn't seem to mind the memory.

She smiled. "She was."

The wine arrived, and after two glasses were poured, Gage lifted his glass. "Let's toast to your mother, Gianna."

"Let's." She picked up her glass and touched his with a soft clink. "To my mom and to yours," she said. "The best women I've ever known."

"Me, too," he said. After they sipped, Gage put down his glass. "You said you were here several times."

"My best friend, Brooke, set me up on a blind date, and he took me here. We dated for a short time, and then he brought me here to break it off."

"Wow. That's cold."

"Not really. He was a nice guy, and he knew I liked this place. It just didn't work out between us. We didn't mesh. He was into sports and cars. His big dream was to go to a baseball game in every ballpark in America."

"A real dud, huh." As a boy, Gage had that very same dream. He'd pitched on his high school varsity team, but then he got the music bug and it had become his passion. He found he could play guitar pretty well, and the deep pitch of his voice worked well with the songs he chose to sing. But he still loved baseball, watched it on TV and played it whenever he could get his bandmates on the field. "So, no sports or cars." She wasn't much into fashion or the latest trends. Gage got the feeling his sister, Lily, was totally responsible for her wardrobe choices, too. "What do you like, Gianna, besides books?"

"I like teaching."

"A given."

"I like ice cream."

"Three scoops, got that. What else?"

"I'm on the board of the Learning and Literacy Foundation at the university. It's a charity to help promote reading. It's a passion of mine. There's a lot of children out there really struggling to read. The university does its fair share of fund-raising."

"Great cause. But do you do anything for fun? Just for the hell of it?"

"I used to travel. Until my mom got sick. That all stopped, but I imagine I'll do it again at some point."

"We're going to do some traveling together. I've got a trip planned to Nashville after the Fourth. And then on to Los Angeles."

"And it's imperative that I go with you?" she asked, looking at him over the rim of her wineglass.

"It's necessary, Gianna."

He had to be blunt. None of this would work if she didn't take these trips with him. It's what she'd signed up for, but if she put up too much of a fuss, he'd have to make some allowances. "There's some great history in Nashville. It's not all about music. I promise to make it bearable."

"After the Fourth, I'll be deep in research for the Family Studies seminar I'm giving at the university at the end of the month. It's a study of major theories regarding family development and delves into the biological, psychological and historical factors that influence family patterns and behavior."

"In English, please?"

Her mouth formed an adorable pout. "Never mind. Just know that while we're on the road, I'll be working in the separate bedroom you promised me, when I'm not with you."

"Fair enough. And speaking of the Fourth, will you agree to be my temporary fiancée, Gianna?" He dipped into his pocket, covering his hand completely over the ring box.

She smiled a beautiful smile. "You have a way with words, Gage."

"I want you to have the ring tonight, but you don't have to wear it until the Fourth. I thought it would be less awkward for you than having me get down on one knee in front of everyone at the party. This way, it's an announcement instead of the actual proposal. And if anyone asks, you can tell them I proposed to you tonight and gave you the ring over dinner at the Rhinestone Room. It wouldn't be a lie. You can keep your committed relationship with the truth." He smiled.

She smiled, too. "I appreciate that and it makes sense."

"Thank you again for doing this." He closed his hand over the ring box and placed it into her palm. Her fingers curled around it, keeping it out of view, and she immediately tucked it into her purse.

"Oh, and there's just one more thing." He reached into his other pocket and came up with a gold velvet drawstring jewelry bag. "This goes with the ring." He slid the bag across the table. "For you, Gianna."

Surprise lit in her eyes. "What's this?"

"Open it."

She stared at him a second and then picked up the bag, looking a bit wary. She undid the drawstring and pulled out the necklace. "It's beautiful," she whispered in awe.

A dozen small diamonds forming a vee dropped down to a single strand that held one delicate marquise diamond. Jeffrey had called it a drop necklace.

She ran the necklace over her palm, the delicate strand caressing her fingers. Her expression changed instantly, and her awe dissolved. "I can't accept this, Gage."

"It'll look perfect on you, Gianna. And yes, you can accept it."

"I'll just have to return it to you when I return the diamond ring."

"All sales are final. Otherwise Jeffrey would have a heart attack."

Gianna's eyes widened. "Are you saying you can't return it?"

"I'm saying…yes. It's unreturnable. Don't you like it?"

"I…love it. But it's too much."

"Let me be the judge of that."

"How did you do this, anyway? When?"

"Let's just say, Jeffrey showed it to me after you walked out of the store. He and I both agreed it would look great on you."

She snapped her fingers. "And just like that, you bought it."

"Yeah."

Gage hadn't been totally unselfish in buying that necklace. He wanted Gianna to have it because of the unorthodox favor she was doing for him. But it was also a way to keep her invested in this scheme. One good turn deserved another. He was asking a lot of her, and he needed to keep her onboard. He wasn't buying her loyalty, but rather showing her how much her sacrifice meant to him. At least, he hoped she viewed it that way.

He couldn't afford for anything to go wrong.

His livelihood depended upon it.

It depended on her.

Gianna wasn't thrilled with Gage's gift, but she kept her irritation to a simmer. They were out in public, and she didn't want to blow her cover. She had given her word to be in this charade until the very end. But she hadn't asked for jewelry—she hadn't asked for anything in return for her favor. Okay, it made sense that he'd give her a ring. She needed to show up at the party wearing it when they made their engagement announcement, but the necklace? That was a different story.

She was more than mildly insulted that Gage thought he had to buy her off with diamonds. She'd like to think otherwise of him, but there was no other logical explanation for him going to such extremes. She ventured to guess the necklace was far more expensive than the ring she'd picked out. Why did he do it? Did he have so little faith in her?

Before she could stop him, he rose from his chair and took the necklace from her hand.

"Allow me," he said.

Baffled, she simply sat there at the table while Gage came around to rest his hand on her shoulder. Gently, he brushed her hair to one side, the backs of his fingers caressing her throat ever so softly. She drew breath into her lungs at his touch, and tingles of awareness flitted through her belly. While his hands worked the clasp, she sat stiffly, perplexed at her reaction to him, to his unnerving presence behind her. She couldn't let him see how he affected her. When he was through and the necklace was fastened, he arranged her hair back in place, his fingers grazing her skin once again. She squeezed her eyes closed briefly, holding her breath.

He sat down, eyeing the drop necklace that landed in the hollow between her breasts. His baby blues lingered long enough to heat her body and make her squirm a bit, not from annoyance this time but from something much more dangerous.

"Gianna, it's perfect on you."

He sounded sincere. No matter what his motives, she couldn't deny the necklace was a beauty. "Thank you."

All during dinner, Gage's eyes dipped down to her breasts. Was he only admiring the gift he'd given her? She surely hoped so. There was no room in her heart for anything else. She was filled with grief, still mourning the passing of her dear mother. Besides, the notion of anything happening between her and Gage in real life was ridiculous. Even if his touch brought flutters. She hadn't been intimate with a man for quite some time, so of course the first bit of contact again would give her butterflies.

Gage poured her a second glass of wine and they spent time talking about him, his concerts, what to expect when they were on the road. Gianna's head began to swim, but she continued to drink, only because Gage was a master storyteller and she actually enjoyed hearing about his antics with his siblings and bandmates. The more she drank, the funnier his stories became, but then suddenly, Gage stopped talking.

"What's wrong?" she asked, swaying a bit. Suddenly, it was hard to focus her eyes. "Tell me m-more."

"Geesh, Gianna, you're a lightweight," Gage said, staring at her. "What'd you have, two and a half glasses of wine?"

"Something like th-that. I'm not much of a drinker."

"I can see that," he muttered. "I'd better get you home."

"I don't want to go h-home." She sounded like a child, but she didn't care.

"Exactly why I need to get you home."

Next, she was being lifted out of her seat and ushered through the restaurant. She smiled at people as she passed by, Gage hurrying her along. He held her tight, his strength kind of a turn-on, and then she was in his car and being buckled in. The air around her was heavy with masculine musk. "Mmm. I l-like the way you smell."

"I'll remember that."

After that, everything was a blur. Houses passed her by. She couldn't stop giggling, even when her eyes were closed. And then, again, Gage had her in his arms. First, they were outside and now they were inside. And she was on a bed, a soft, cozy bed, and her eyes slowly opened.

"Gage?"

"Get some sleep. I'll check on you in the morning."

Her hair was brushed aside, and she felt his lips on her forehead.

She lifted her arms, grabbing for him. "Don't g-go."

He broke away from her, setting her arms down gently. "Got to, Brainiac."

She giggled and then closed her eyes again.

And drifted off.

Morning broke through the windows in Gianna's bedroom, the sunlight penetrating the gaps in the shutters. Her lids were like lead, too heavy to open right now. The light was too bright. She needed the dark. All she wanted to do was sleep off her pounding headache.

She let out a long, low groan of pain, but that wasn't the only reason the grotesque noise rumbled up from her chest. What she could remember of last night gave her hives. She'd made a blubbering fool out of herself at dinner. Gage had had to hold her tight, his arm propping her up as they left the restaurant, and Lord only knew what on earth she'd said to him on the drive home. Or worse yet, what she'd said to him as he'd tucked her into bed.

"Oh, man," she muttered. She was supposed to be the stable, responsible one of the pair and not act like a drunken roadie. She prayed no one snapped a picture of her, or worse yet, took video as she left the Rhinestone Room with Gage. This was not the image she wanted to portray. As all sorts of humiliating scenarios played out in her mind, she dug herself deeper down into the covers.

Gage's voice rang out on her cell phone. A song about a brokenhearted woman. She didn't know the tune, but Gage had assured her it was one of his biggest hits, and it would be only natural to have his ringtone on her cell phone. He had even done the honors of changing it for her yesterday.

Still prone on her bed, she rummaged through her purse on the nightstand and came up with her phone. Another groan escaped her throat as Brooke's face popped up. Gianna debated answering the call or not, but knowing her best friend, she'd probably call her back every five minutes until she answered.

"Hello," she whispered, the shallow sound of her voice making her cringe.

"Do I have to be the last one to know?" Brooke said.

Her mind was cloudy enough without having to guess anything. "To know what?"

"That you're dating Gage Tremaine."

Gianna sat upright on the bed, forgetting about the ache in her head. She hadn't yet figured out how to explain this to her best friend, or if she even should. "Why do you think that?"

"Is it true, Gia?"

"Well, uh…tell me why you think that?"

"You were seen with him at Triple Scoop. And last night, you had dinner with him at the Rhinestone Room, for heaven's sake. It's been all over social media."

It's exactly what Gage's manager wanted. The social media buzz meant their little plan was working. But Brooke was a true-blue friend, and she hated lying to her. Gianna didn't know if she could, especially since their engagement announcement would make big news tomorrow.

"I can explain all that." But could she? Could she explain away her phony relationship with Gage? Her mind wasn't clear enough to make that decision now.

"I'm listening."

"I can't really talk right now. Someone took a sledgehammer to my head," she whispered. "I drank too much last night. I can barely focus on anything. Can I call you later?"

Brooke hesitated. "Are you…okay, Gianna?"

Brooke knew she'd been having trouble accepting her mother's passing. And her friend had been regularly checking in on her, making sure she was managing. "Because if you need me, I'll come right over."

"Thank you. You're the best, but I'll be fine."

"But Gage, Gia? That worries me. He's so…not

your type. I know he's hot, and has those killer blue eyes, but honestly, I hope your explanation doesn't include romance with that guy."

It didn't. At least she could admit that. Gianna would never fall for a guy like Gage. And her reasons were justified, the secret she held wouldn't allow it. "We'll talk. I'll get myself together and call you later. I promise."

"Okay, we'll talk later," Brooke said, sounding a bit more relieved. "Take care of yourself."

"I will." Gianna ended the call and silenced the ringer. She wanted no more interruptions. She laid her head onto the pillow and tried to relax. Not five minutes later, there was a knock on her door.

"Go away," she muttered. She ducked her head under the covers, needing peace and not an unwanted visitor. But it could be Rose. And Gianna didn't want to ignore her if she was the one the knocking.

She got up very slowly and sat a second, gathering her wits, allowing her head to adjust to the upright position. It was idiotic that two glasses of wine could do this to her. *Never again*, she vowed and rose, gently donning a well-worn chenille bathrobe.

The knocking grew louder, and then she heard Gage's voice from behind the door. "Gianna, it's Gage."

She bit her lip. She didn't want to see him. She didn't want *him* to see her in this state, either. "Gage, what are you doing here?" she asked, just behind the door.

"Helping. Let me in."

"I don't need your help."

"I have the key."

Her shoulders slumped. Of course he had the key. He came prepared. He had been a Boy Scout once, after all.

"That's blackmail."

"It's me helping. Open the door, Gianna."

She put her hand on the knob, pursed her lips and then slowly cracked the door.

Gage came bearing gifts. And not of the diamond variety this time. The coffeepot on the tray smelled good, solid and strong. He'd also brought a bottle of aspirin. She could use both items about now.

She stepped away from the door, and he moved inside, heading for the kitchen. "I'd ask you how you're feeling, but your face says it all."

"Compliments, so early in the morning."

His mouth crooked up, and he eyed the ratty robe she was wearing. He might as well have told her she looked like something the cat dragged in, with that expression. He took her hand, dropped two aspirin in her palm and handed her half a glass of water. "Take them."

She did.

Next, he poured coffee into two cups and set them on the table. His hands came to her shoulders and pointed her toward the kitchen chair. "Sit."

She lowered down slowly and lifted her coffee mug, breathing in the aroma before taking a sip. Hot coffee was just what she needed. She knew enough that coffee didn't really dilute the alcohol, but it sure tasted good going down. Lucky for her, her tummy was fine. It was the gremlins stomping on her head that hurt the most.

Gage sat, too. He took a plate of plain toast off the tray and put it her under her nose. "Can you eat?"

"Should I? I mean, you're the expert on hangovers."

His mouth twisted, but his eyes were soft with pity. She hated that he pitied her.

"Am I? I certainly can handle much more than a thimble of wine."

"I have no doubt."

"Did you sleep all night?"

"Up until some rude person began pounding on my door."

"It's ten o'clock in the morning, Gianna. And you should be thanking me for bringing you remedies. It's obvious you don't know how to help yourself."

"So, I'm not an expert on hangovers."

"'Bout the only thing you don't think you're an expert on."

She bit into her toast and chewed and chewed. It was as dry as straw, and she washed it down with coffee. She was in a foul mood because her head ached, but also because she didn't remember what had happened last night, exactly. And she hated being out of control.

"You're wrong. I'm not an expert on fake engagements, either, so forgive me if I overindulged."

"You're forgiven."

She ground her teeth. Which only made her head ache more.

"Actually, I sorta liked you all loose and giddy." Gage took a sip of coffee. "Makes me think there's more to you than I originally thought."

"More to me?"

"Yeah, a fun side of you."

"Fun?" What did he mean by that? She couldn't recall the end of the night. And it bugged the stuffing out of her. "What made you think that?"

He grabbed a piece of toast, took a bite and chewed, making her wait. She wasn't sure she wanted to hear his answer. And yet she had to know.

"I carried you into the bedroom and laid you down on the bed."

Oh, man.

"And when I said good-night to you, you asked me not to go."

A chuckle burst out of her chest, as if he'd said the sky was green. Actually, that notion was more conceivable. "No way. I'd never say that to you."

Gage's brows lifted, and an earnest expression crossed his features, as if…as if he wasn't lying. Then his mouth twitched, in the teasing way he had. "You're right, Gianna. You didn't say that."

But last night, she did recall the feel of his breath against her throat, his hands in her hair and the gentle way he'd fastened the diamond necklace from behind. His touch made her nerves rattle. Made her aware of his masculinity. The scent of his cologne had been strong then, and now there was a hint of it still wafting to her nostrils. She remembered her heart pounding when his hands had been on her shoulders. Even now, the scent of him threatened to make her weak.

But it wasn't like Gage to concede so soon, and now she truly wondered. "I kn-know. I wouldn't."

Would she?

But one thing was certain—this was the last time she was going to let loose like that. She wouldn't give Gage the upper hand again.

No matter his striking appeal.

Or how his bluer than blue eyes could melt her.

Three

"Nobody has to know the truth, Cade. Just the family," Gage remarked to his brother on the morning of the Fourth. Later this evening, the real fireworks would begin for him and Gianna.

"I don't like Harper being in on your charade. She's had enough negative press to last a lifetime."

Cade sat down at the kitchen table, a hot cup of coffee steaming right in front of him. It was natural for his brother to feel protective of his fiancée. They'd had a bumpy road finding each other, and Harper had been put through the wringer with bad press. At one point, Harper had been the most hated reality star in the country. But it had all worked out in the end. And if all went well with Regan's little scheme, no one would be the wiser. Once the summer was over, Gage's high-profile engagement would fade into oblivion, his reputation would hopefully be restored, and then a low-key breakup would follow.

"I didn't ask her to cater the event, Cade. She offered to help. Besides, I don't see how we could avoid telling her the truth. We couldn't lie to her."

"That's right, Cade. I'm glad I know the truth. And I volunteered to help with the food on my own." Harper sat down next to her fiancé and took his hand. "I'm a chef and if I want to do this for your family," she said softly, "I'm *going* to do it. And as far as the charade goes, in a few months, I'll officially be a Tremaine, so I'm all in." She kissed Cade on the cheek. "You don't have to worry about me, sweetheart. I don't feel offended. I feel *included*."

Gage gave his brother a shrug, trying not to appear glib. He liked Harper. She had spunk and was the perfect match for his uptight brother. Cade had never been happier, and it showed.

"All right, I hear both of you. We'll play along until the end." Cade sipped coffee and picked up a biscuit. "But don't you go thinking about catering our wedding day, sweetheart. That day, I want you all to myself."

"I wouldn't dream of it. I really can't wait for that day to come."

"Me, too."

Cade gave his fiancée a solid kiss that lasted long enough for Gage to wonder if he'd ever fall head over heels in love with a woman. He'd never really loved a woman before, not the way his father had loved his mother. Not the way Cade loved Harper. His relationships with women weren't heavy or powerful. Mostly, he didn't have time to devote to making one woman that important to him. His father's words rang in his ears every time he'd think about getting serious—"It's not the woman you can live with, it's the woman you can't live without."

So far, Gage hadn't met a woman he couldn't live without. And he wondered if it was him. Was he incapable of loving that hard, that powerfully?

"Now, both of you need to give me some space. I've got my team coming in to prep for the day." Harper gestured with a sweep of her hands. "Let the chef do her work."

Gage rose and kissed Harper on the cheek. "You fit into this family already, Harp. Thanks for everything you're doing. I'll see you later."

She gave him a big smile. Gage had never thought he'd be envious of Cade, not in the female department for sure, but something jabbed him right smack in the heart every time Cade's eyes lit as soon as Harper walked into the room.

Cade had the real thing.

While Gage was only pretending.

Gage walked past the parlor and spied his mother sitting in her chair reading the newspaper. He did an immediate about-face, but he wasn't quick enough.

"Gage, a word, please," she said, catching him ducking out.

"Ah, sure, Mom." He gave her a big smile, one that

probably hadn't fooled her since his teenage days. "What can I do for you?"

"Have a seat."

He sat down on the sofa in the giant living room. It was the centerpiece of the entire house, a room with tall beveled-glass windows, polished wood flooring, a floor-to-ceiling stone fireplace and various sitting areas throughout the space. His mother liked to call the decor "rustic elegance." And the Texas estate suited her style: character and charm with country flair. Gage had always loved this room. It reminded him of his father and the hard work he'd put in to be able to build this house for his family. But at this exact moment, he felt more like a schoolboy being summoned into the principal's office.

"It's a big day today," Rose said, a master of the obvious. "How are you holding up?"

"Me? I'm fine."

Her brows arched, her way of expressing skepticism. "You are? No worries or concerns about your announcement tonight?"

"No, ma'am. I'll be doing just fine."

"So you're sure about this?"

"Yeah, I am," he assured her. His mother had never been keen on the fake engagement idea, yet she'd given him her support, and he wanted to ease her trepidation.

"I hope you are. Because this isn't a small favor you're asking of Gianna. She's been through so much already, caring for Tonette, only to lose her this year. And now she's being thrust into this little charade.

She's a good sport, as you know. You certainly bad-
gered her enough over the years, and she always came
out fighting."

"She points that out every chance she gets," he
said. "The badgering, I mean. I was pretty rough on
her, because she always had to be right. And it bugged
me because she actually was right most of the time.
She really is a brain. But as you said, Gianna is no
wilting flower. She gives as much as she takes."

"I love that about her, Gage. In fact, I love her, period. She's like a second daughter to me. This year
has been especially tough." The edges of his mother's
eyes crinkled as tears welled up. His mom reached
for his hand. "I'm trusting you, Gage. To be good to
Gianna. I wouldn't want to see her hurt again, by any
means. I know she's intelligent, but she's also very
vulnerable right now. I need your promise now that
you'll be mindful of that. You'll be careful with her.
Don't lead her down a path—"

"Mom, you have nothing to worry about." Gage
figured his mother would be protective of Gianna.
They had a strong bond, but her worries weren't justified. Gianna might look pretty in a dress and a new
hairstyle, but he knew his place. She was helping him
out of a jam, and that's all there was to it. Nothing
more. "I'll be careful, and if it'll make you sleep better at night, I can tell you, Gianna and I are complete
opposites. We don't jell, and she'd be the first one to
tell you that. So put your worries to rest. At the very
least, Gianna will be too distracted to be sad over her
mama's death. And at the very best, she'll be able to

travel some. She hasn't been able to do that for quite a few years, and she misses it."

His mother sighed heavily. "That does make me feel better, Gage. I needed your promise on this, son."

"You have it. I'll take good care of Gianna."

"Thank you." She folded up the newspaper and laid it down. "That's what I needed to hear." His mother stood, and Gage rose as well. "Now it's time to check with Lily about the plans for tonight's barbecue. I'm hoping all is under control. I'm getting excited. Our guests will be arriving for the party in less than four hours."

Gage smiled. His mom loved the annual Tremaine Fourth of July party. It was her way of celebrating the holiday with family and friends in their community while honoring the birth of the country. And tonight, he'd make the announcement to the world that he and Gianna were in love and getting married.

Suddenly, reality bit him in the ass. He'd made a lot of promises to a lot of people in the past, but the one he'd just made to his mother was one he had to uphold.

No matter what.

Gage stood behind Gianna's door, wishing he didn't have to do this. Wishing there was some other way. She wasn't going to like it, and that was a gross understatement. What he wanted to do was grab his suitcase and head on back to the main house, but his back was against the wall, and he couldn't turn and run like he wanted to do.

Instead, he braved a knock on her door, holding his breath. Gianna opened it seconds later. "Gage, what are you doing here? You're four hours early."

Not by choice, he wanted to say as his brows rose at her appearance. She wore baggy gray sweats with Fairmont University Tigers printed in bold letters on her shirt. Her hair was in a tight twisty thing at the top of her head, her glasses were nearly on the tip of her nose and a ballpoint pen was tucked behind her ear.

"I know. Something's come up. Am I interrupting?" He looked over her shoulder, finding her computer screen flashing.

"Yes, actually you are. I'm in the middle of my research project for the upcoming seminar."

"You're working?" He found it incredible that Gianna could focus on work today. Didn't most women spend half the day getting ready for an important occasion? And this wasn't just any occasion, but the day they would announce their engagement to the world. A day that would change Gianna's entire life. At least temporarily.

"You can see that I am." Her eyes drew down to his suitcase curiously. "Are you going someplace?" Then she smiled. "I know, you've given up on this whole crazy idea and you're off on some wild vacation."

Didn't that sound like fun? "Not even close."

He leaned against her door frame. "My band surprised me and showed up for the Fourth of July bash. Whenever they're in town, they know they have a place to stay here. Toby, Lionel and Paolo usually stay in the guesthouse."

"So, what's the problem? They'll stay at the main house, right?"

Gage scrubbed his jaw. "Right. Yep. That's where they're staying, but—"

"Wait a minute. You're not planning on moving in here." She began shaking her head adamantly, her eyes as round as silver dollars. "Tell me that's not what your luggage on the doorstep is all about."

"I knew with your quick wit, you'd figure it out."

"No. No. Not gonna happen, Gage. Are you crazy?" She folded her arms across her middle.

"Gianna, we're supposed to be in love and getting married. If I sleep in the house, the guys are gonna know something's up. Don't worry. Stay where you are and I'll take one of the other bedrooms."

She glared at him, but he didn't have time to waste. "Sorry. I can't stand out here arguing with you." Gage grabbed his suitcase and strode past her, entering the house. She remained at the front door, in disbelief.

He turned to her. "It's either this or you move into my bedroom with me at the main house. There's only one bed in my room—granted, it's pretty big," he said, the innuendo clear. Oddly, he visualized Gianna naked in his bed waiting for him, her hair spilling down her shoulders and caressing her soft skin, her eyes filled with yearning.

Get a grip, Gage.

Oh, man, after having that conversation with his mother, he should be struck down by lightning for giving any credence to that notion.

"Not on your life." Right on cue, Gianna set him straight.

"So, I'll take the far bedroom," he said.

Gianna shut the front door, her mouth in a pout. "Fine."

His shoulders slumped. The Gianna he knew never made things easy for him, and if this was how it was going to be from now on, he was in for a mighty long summer.

"Just don't make it a habit of surprising me with this kind of thing," she said.

"You know when we go on the road, we'll be staying in a hotel room together, right?"

"I'm aware," she said, her chin pointed up. "But you promised me a suite with two rooms."

"You'll have that, Gianna."

"Okay, then. I've really got to get back to work."

That was Gianna. Always with her nose in a book or her head in the computer.

That didn't seem to bother him right now. But what did was that her appearance in shapeless clothes and uncombed hair no longer turned him off.

Because he knew what was hidden underneath all those less-than-appealing trappings.

And he wasn't just talking about her sexy-as-sin body. Some might say her brilliant mind was a big turn-on. Not him, of course. But suddenly he was grateful she didn't like him all that much. Suddenly, he was glad she looked upon him with disdain at times.

"Go, Gianna," he told her. "Get back to what you were doing. You won't even know I'm here."

"No more interruptions?"

"None. We'll head over to the house about four o'clock. How's that?"

She sighed. "I'll be ready."

He stared into Gianna's pretty green eyes as they shared a moment of deep acknowledgment. Their little charade was about to begin.

And very soon, they'd be under the spotlight together.

Everything from here on out would be one big, fat lie.

Four

Gianna walked out of her bedroom, fully dressed for the Fourth of July barbecue, and found Gage standing in the front room, gazing out the window. From the back, he looked pretty stellar in black jeans and a matching Western shirt embroidered along the shoulders with a swirling pattern that ran down his sleeves. He wore a Stetson that he usually called his "John B." Sensing she was in the room, he turned to face her, and the full impact of his appeal hit her smack between the eyes.

Masculine, rugged and handsome. She knew why women fawned over him, aside from the deep tones of his voice. He was the picture of pure country male.

He gave her outfit a look, and a smile lifted the corners of his mouth. "Wow," he said, "you look—"

"Patriotic?"

Gage shook his head. "Very pretty, Gianna."

"Thanks. Lily's doing again." Gianna didn't want to overdress for the occasion. To everyone else in attendance, it was simply an Independence Day celebration, so she'd wanted to keep with the theme instead of going too fancy. Her off-the-shoulder white dress was tiered with lace on its bell sleeves and also at the hem just above her knees. The scoop neck had a drawstring pull that Lily insisted she tie loosely, allowing for a deep dip at the chest. Gianna thought the look too bold, but there was no arguing with Lily. She knew fashion. A wide silver belt decorated with turquoise stones and a choker of the same design completed the outfit, along with a red cowgirl hat and matching leather boots. "I never would've put this together," she said honestly.

"Oh, so you've never been line dancing?" Gage grinned.

Horrified, she blinked. "Is that what I look like?"

"Only ten times better. And just right for the party tonight. The hat's a nice touch."

She touched the brim, sliding her fingers along the edge. "It's not me. I'm not a hat person."

"I'd say you are. Hats make a statement. Takes a confident woman to wear one. And that's you."

She wasn't entirely sure of that, but she could pretend. This whole night was about faking it, so what was one more thing to fake? "Well, you look nice, too."

He shrugged. "Not my Sunday best, but something fittin' for a party."

Or one of his concerts. She'd seen him wear flashy clothes like that onstage.

He glanced at his watch. "It's just about time to go."

She put her head down, regrouping. This was it. Her nerves rattling, her heart pounding, she prayed she could pull off the deception. She'd given her word and she couldn't back out, so she lifted her lids to Gage and nodded. "Let's do this."

Gage studied her a minute, his gaze sharp and steady. Then the dark hue of his eyes softened, and in a true honest moment, he said, "Thank you."

He put out his hand and entwined their fingers. They exited the guesthouse together, strolling up the road to where the backyard grounds were transformed with patriotic balloons, streamers and bunting. There was a dance floor set up, and tables and chairs. Music was piped in, and Gage explained that his band wasn't scheduled to play, but they might put together a few songs later on in the evening. Barbecues and smokers sent a spicy, delectable aroma throughout the property.

Rose was the first to greet them. She gave Gianna a hug and kiss on the cheek and then did the same to Gage. Cade and Harper were busy speaking with a bartender at the backyard bar. Lily was there chatting with Nathan, the Tremaine horse wrangler. Guests were starting to arrive. Gianna recognized a few of them, having been to many of the Tremaines' parties in the past.

Toby, Leo and Paolo walked up. Gianna had met them before, but she couldn't recall who was who. One of them slapped their lead singer on the back, wearing a big smile. "Hey, Gage. You're holding out on us. Who's this pretty lady?"

"This is Gianna Marino. You've met before," Gage said, "at least once or twice backstage."

Gage put his arm around Gianna's waist and drew her close. The move surprised her, and she forced a big smile. Gage held her possessively and their bodies meshing together created goose bumps on her arms. "Gianna, this is Leo. He's our lead guitarist. And Paolo over here, with the rat's nest beard, is the best drummer Nashville has ever produced." He turned toward a young man with long blond hair. "This is Toby. He plays the fiddle."

"Hi, guys," she said. "Nice seeing you again."

Each one appeared puzzled, as if they couldn't place her. Had her appearance changed that much? "Same here," Toby said. "I do remember you now. You're a family friend, right? You came backstage one night with Rose and your mother."

"Yes, that's right. My mother, Tonette, was with us that night."

She felt Gage's muscles tense up. He shifted a bit. "Gianna lost her mother a short time ago," he said, as if warning them to drop the subject.

"Sorry to hear that," Toby said, and the others muttered their condolences as well.

"Gianna is more than a family friend," Gage said, looking at her with adoring eyes. "We're together now."

Gage's band members hid their reactions well. If they'd seen anything about them on social media, they didn't acknowledge it.

"Cool," Leo said, and the others politely agreed. She felt them assessing her, and she wasn't sure if they were buying it. They'd toured with Gage for years, knew him pretty well and knew his taste in women. To her knowledge, Gage had never had a serious relationship. He must hate lying to his band members, but they'd agreed that only those who absolutely had to know the truth would be told. The lie was too much of a burden for their friends to carry.

Gage motioned toward the bar. "You boys ready for a drink? The bartender is making some sort of Independence Day explosion up at the bar."

"As long as they have whiskey straight up, I'm good," Paolo said.

"Well, an explosion sounds pretty dang good to me." Toby grinned. "Think I'll try one."

"You boys go on, and we'll see you in a bit. I'm glad you all made it tonight." He winked. "Gonna be a special night all the way around."

The three took off, and just as Gage was steering her toward Cade and Harper, a female voice called out from behind them. "Gage."

Gage and Gianna turned in unison. "Regan? You made it," he said, puzzled. "I thought you got held up in Nashville."

Gage's manager's face was flushed as she approached, her blond hair falling from the pins that held it up. She wore a gorgeous sapphire-blue dress that hit just above the knees, a stunning ruby necklace draping her throat and white designer slingbacks. "I did—almost didn't make the flight."

Gage released Gianna to give his fortysomething manager a big hug. He seemed genuinely pleased to see her. "Well, I appreciate the effort. Sorry about the trouble you went through."

"It's okay. It's my job…anything for you," she said, her eyes sparkling. She turned to Gianna. "I almost didn't recognize you." She looked Gianna up and down, her mouth in a bit of pout as if she were measuring her up, making sure she was fit to be the country superstar's fiancée. Then, as if she passed inspection, Regan smiled. "Are you all set for this, Gianna?"

"As ready as I'll ever be, I guess."

"Gage and I appreciate you doing this."

There was something in the way she spoke, rather possessively, that Gianna thought odd. But then, the woman had been Gage's manager and mentor for most of his career. If anyone had the right to look out for Gage, it would be her. "I need a private moment with Gage, if you don't mind," his manager told her. "It's business."

Gianna stiffened. The last thing she wanted was to face the crowd alone.

"Can we do it later, Regan?" Gage asked.

"Not really. We need to nail a few things down

regarding your schedule. You know how hard I've worked on setting it up." She looked at Gianna. "It's boring stuff, and I promise it'll only take a few minutes. You understand, right?"

Gage was nodding his head, encouraging her, so she took his cue. "Of course."

"Thanks. Maybe you could go talk with Lily," he said, relieved. "This shouldn't take too long."

"Sure. You go on. I'll be fine." Suddenly, she was fully aware where she placed in Gage's pecking order. His career came first, that was a given, but she hadn't expected him to abandon her tonight. They were to portray a unified front. At least while in the public eye.

Luckily, Lily was heading her way, and the two joined up over by the pool area, where red, white and blue candles floated in the water, ready to be lit as soon as the sun went down.

"Wow, you look fantastic, Gianna," Lily said. "That outfit really works for you."

"That's only because you do excellent exterior work. And I love your dress, too." It was an off-the-shoulder cherry-red dress that flounced when she walked and suited Lily's personality perfectly.

"I bet my brother flipped when he saw you. Where is he, anyway?" Lily scanned the grounds for him. "I thought I saw you two together a few minutes ago."

"You did. We were just joining the party, but Regan had some important business to discuss with him."

"Tonight?" Lily sighed. "I swear, that woman

never lets up. She shouldn't have dragged him away tonight of all nights."

That's what Gianna thought, too. "But she's helping him repair his reputation, so she has a vested interest in him."

"That, or some other interest, but let's not go there. How about we go grab a drink? You have to try the Explosion. I hear it's amazing."

Gianna didn't question her cryptic comment. Gage's relationship with Regan was none of her business, and she wanted to keep it that way. "How about I have a sip of yours? I need to keep my wits about me tonight."

"Sure." Then Lily linked their arms and led her toward the bar.

Gianna was too much of a lightweight to master a drink blended with several types of liquor. The last time she had too much wine, according to Gage, she'd thrown herself at him. Asked him not to leave her bedside.

But when she called bullshit on him, he'd given in too easily. Which made her wonder about his motives. About her innermost desires.

When all her inhibitions were gone, did she secretly have a thing for her soon-to-be fake fiancé?

As the sun began to set, Gianna found her place at the Tremaine table along with Gage, Rose, Cade, Harper and the band members. Brisket was a given at a Texas barbecue, and Gianna watched Gage eat up heartily. He had a heaping plate filled with beans and coleslaw and hush puppies. Laughter filled the air, everyone having a good time eating and conversing. There were at least eighty people here, maybe more. Harper had told her the guest list topped one hundred, and guests were still strolling in, finding the bar and buffet line easily enough.

Gianna had been to these Tremaine parties before and had always felt a bit left out. She wasn't one for big crowds—unless they were her students in a lecture hall—or making small talk to people she'd just met. There were politicians here, the mayor of Juliet, as well as CEOs of big oil companies. Ranchers and rodeo riders, people who defined Texas high society, were dressed accordingly in big hats and belt buckles and thousand-dollar leather boots. According to Regan, news reporters were here under direct orders to steer clear of all the guests, use discretion and photograph the party from a distance. She'd promised them an interview with Gage after the celebration was over.

Gianna never felt comfortable at these kinds of shindigs. She wasn't a snob, but rather a misfit, a girl who'd rather have her nose in a book than be the life of the party. A Texan who loved to learn and loved to teach. She must've appeared a little befuddled, her dinner plate barely touched, because Gage covered her hand with his and gave her a smile. It was a heart-melter, one he was practiced at, but it did manage to calm her quivering nerves. He leaned in and spoke into her ear. "I'll make our announcement right after supper," he said.

She nodded and pulled back to gaze into his eyes. He winked, as if this was all some sort of carefree game. Sure, *his* life wasn't going to change. His life would stay the same, while she was tasked with going along for the ride—*his ride*.

Her mama's image popped into her mind. She had been a gentle lady with nothing but love in her heart. Oh, how Gianna missed her. It had been the two of them against the world, it seemed, for the longest time. But Rose had been there, too, always a friend, always with a kind word to ease her mother's burden. Her mama had loved all the Tremaines, and she would have wanted her to help Gage. She'd be proud of the sacrifice Gianna was making to help out a friend. The thought brought comfort and made sense of this whole thing.

Thirty minutes later, dinner was winding down, and the dishes were being cleared. "I'm ready," she told Gage. She gazed down at the engagement ring she'd just put on her finger. She hadn't wanted to wear it, until absolutely necessary. It sorta made the lie she was living a little easier to take.

Gage squeezed her hand, and an electric jolt seized her for a second. She stared at Gage's smiling face and smiled back.

Gage pulled her along, past the dance floor and up onto a little stage they had set up. The party was in full swing.

Harper and Regan made sure everyone had a flute of champagne in their hand as Gage assessed the group, gave the cue to shut down the music and then picked up the microphone. "Hey, everyone. On behalf of my mother, Rose, and all the Tremaines, I want to thank you for celebrating this special night with us."

At the sound of Gage's voice, everyone dropped what they were doing and turned toward the stage to listen. Gianna felt all eyes shift from him to her as guests curiously wondered what she was doing onstage with him.

"It's the birth of our nation. The good ole US of A. Our Independence Day. And that's certainly something great to celebrate."

Cheers went up all the way around.

"But it's also the day I'm happily losing my independence." He turned to Gianna, his blue eyes arrowed straight at her. "Everyone, this beautiful woman beside me is Professor Gianna Marino. We've known each other since forever. And…well, I'm crazy about her. Lucky for me, Gianna feels the same way. I've asked Gianna to marry me, and she said yes, so I'm here to announce that Gianna and I are engaged."

Gasps of surprise filled the yard. Many cheered and some applauded. Gianna smiled, but she was afraid she came off as too timid. Gage laced a possessive arm around her waist, drawing her extremely close. Then he turned to face her, his eyes heated and darkened to midnight blue. The pounding in her chest escalated. He leaned forward, tilting her head up, alerting her of his intent. She braced herself, her heart hammering, racing so darn fast. He was going to kiss her right here onstage in front of a hundred pairs of eyes.

And at the first touch of his delicious mouth on hers, she stilled. Breath froze in her throat. She couldn't seem to form a rational thought. But Gage had mastered the art of seduction, and the shock ebbed quickly, replaced by a slow, hot burn, rocking her, tossing her off balance. It was crazy how his lips, meshed with hers, could elicit such instant heat. She fell deeply into the kiss, fully absorbing his power, his desire. Sensations swept over her body, unleashing uncanny abandon. She wrapped her arms around his neck, tugging him closer, and he deepened the kiss, claiming her mouth with what seemed like very little effort. A little moan of pleasure escaped her throat, and she could feel Gage smile, his lips curling up as he continued to possess her. His hand around her waist lowered to just above the curve of her buttocks, a place somewhere between decency and too far. It was as if he'd ignited something fiery in her. Everything below her waist burned. Lusty notions she'd never entertained before rushed forth with alarming speed.

Wolf calls and whistles from the guests brought her back to earth. They'd kissed for far too long, and the partygoers were eating it up.

Oh, God.

She popped her eyes open to Gage's handsome face. He stared at her for a long moment, hunger evident in his eyes—and maybe a bit of shock, too. He blinked several times before taking half a step back.

His breathing was as labored as hers. Had he lost

himself, too? Had he been as floored as she'd been to discover the red-hot chemistry between them?

"That was…good," he rasped for her ears only. "Wait till you see what comes next."

Did he mean she'd put on a good display or…

He entwined their fingers and turned both of them toward the guests.

News reporters rushed toward the stage, snapping photos and shouting questions. For half a second there, Gianna had forgotten why she was here. She'd forgotten their little ruse. For half a second, she'd felt connected to another person in a way she'd never felt before. A sigh escaped her throat, and she turned away from the crowd to look at Gage again.

He was grinning, holding her close, posing them both for the cameras.

A loud boom made her jump, and all eyes lifted upward. Rockets soared skyward, and red, white and blue fireworks illuminated the hills behind the Tremaine estate. They exploded in succession, splashing the heavens with brilliant color as patriotic music played in the background. It was the perfect ending to their little charade, something no one in attendance would soon forget.

Gage had wanted to make a big scene, and he'd sure gotten one. News of their engagement would be cemented in the headlines now. His fans would be happy. This engagement would impact the country music scene and allow Gage the positive publicity he craved.

She was his stabilizer. The woman behind the man.

She had the perfect résumé—a young, stable family friend with a squeaky-clean image and a position at a university.

She was just what the doctor ordered.

Correction—she was just what Gage had ordered.

Oh, Mama, what have I gotten myself into?

After the announcement was made, Gage fielded questions from reporters and posed for a few photos with Gianna right by his side. Most of the questions were regarding his mystery woman, someone who'd come out of the blue to become his fiancée. And while he'd answered those questions as vaguely as possible, being somewhat of an expert at evading the press, he tried to keep his responses as truthful as he could.

He was learning Gianna's body language already. She stiffened every time he was asked a probing question about her. She clearly wasn't comfortable with this line of interrogation.

"Yes, we've known each other since we were children."

"No, we never dated prior to this. I was kind of a thorn in her side, to tell you the truth."

All eyes turned to Gianna. She forced a smile. He was determined to control the dialogue. He wouldn't bring up her mother's recent death. No, he wouldn't use Tonette that way. Or Gianna, for that matter. At all costs, he wanted to keep Gianna's grief out of the public eye. The fact was, she didn't like lying, and neither did he, but this one time it was a must.

"We might've always been a little bit in love, but

it took me getting injured for us to realize our true feelings for each other. My time at home lately made me take stock of my future, and I realized Gianna had to be a part of that future. We're in love and we've wasted enough time being apart."

At least part of that was true. And that killer of a kiss would've definitely convinced any skeptics. Wow, where had all that passion come from? He hadn't expected it. Hadn't given a thought about kissing Gianna in front everyone. Yet, once his mouth claimed hers, he'd been struck by something powerful, something overwhelming. The heat, the chemistry, the burn of desire ripped through him. It wasn't all for show. Oh, it'd started out that way, but a second into the kiss, he was captivated and hungry for more.

Another reporter asked a question, bringing him out of his thoughts.

He answered it, and then Gage dismissed the reporters, asking them to respect his privacy and let them get back to the party.

A few more photos were snapped, and then, to his surprise, no one lingered. The news-hungry reporters were probably eager to get their stories in to their editors for the morning edition. Afterward, Gage and Gianna were congratulated by just about every person at the shindig. He held her hand throughout, keeping her close and doing most of the talking.

Paolo, Toby and Leo joined in to shake his hand and give Gianna a big hug.

Paolo put his hand on Gage's shoulder, nodding

his head in approval. "It's about time this guy settled down."

"Spoken by the only married one in the band."

"Why should I be the only one to suffer?" Paolo grinned and winked at Gianna. "Joking. I love my family. My wife, Jessica, and I just had a baby. It's a boy." He took out his phone and, instantly, a chubby little guy appeared, showing off a big, toothless smile.

"He's adorable," Gianna said, her eyes going soft. "I bet you miss him."

"I do. Every minute. But since we're not touring right now, I can spend a lot of time with him. He'll be six months old next week."

"What's his name?"

"Paolo Jr. But we're calling him Paulie right now."

"That's so cute."

Paolo turned his attention to his bandmate. "Can't wait for you to have a kid."

"A kid? Me?" Gage hadn't thought about having kids. He'd always been career-minded. Yet, seeing Gianna looking adoringly at little chubby cheeks, he could almost imagine it. Maybe. Nah. What was wrong with him? That kiss had rattled his mind. "I have to walk down the aisle first."

"So, when's the wedding?" Toby asked.

Gage had prepared himself for these kinds of questions, but he wasn't sure Gianna had. He wrapped his arm around her waist and dragged her to his side. "We're thinking on it. Right, sugar?" he asked Gianna.

Gianna's brow shot up. She didn't like the endearment. He figured he'd get an earful from her later.

"We still have so much to decide, honey bun." She sent an adoring smile his way.

Gage did a mental eye roll. His quick-witted fake fiancée could go toe to toe with him. He'd almost forgotten. "We'll be sure to let you all know when we decide."

Regan strolled up, and one by one, the guys found an excuse to walk away. They were not her biggest fans, but she'd been loyal and true to him all these years, so he pretty much let it slide.

"It's done," Regan said quietly.

"It sure is."

"You kinda laid it on pretty thick with that kiss." Regan smiled, darting a glance at Gianna, whose cheeks suddenly appeared rosy red. A difficult feat for an olive-skinned Italian girl.

"There should be no room for doubt now," he said.

Gianna flinched, and he envisioned the wheels in her mind turning. He'd come off as callous when he'd really been stunned by the impact of her kiss. Stunned and amazed and pleasantly surprised.

"Anything for the cause," Gianna responded. She toyed with the frames of her glasses. "Guess I'm a good actress after all."

"Guess you are," Gage shot back, irritated.

"Well, there's no turning back now," Regan said, glancing at the both of them. "You're off to the races."

"No, no turning back," Gage repeated, trying to hide his annoyance. Just who was he annoyed at? Himself for being caught so incredibly off guard and enjoying that kiss far too much, or Gianna for making light of it and pretending she wasn't as astonished as he was? "Well, I guess we should get back. Some people are ready to leave."

Regan nodded. "Yes, and I see the mayor and his wife are about to go. I want to catch them before they do." She stepped away and then turned abruptly. "Oh, and keep it up, you two. You're doing great!"

He gave her a nod and she took off, heading back into the fray.

"She's got your back," Gianna said.

"She's a good manager." He paused. "And friend."

"Yes, I can see that."

"You don't approve?" he asked.

"I didn't say that. She concocted this grand plan for you, after all."

"Gianna, if you're upset about something, just lay it on me now. Before we go back to the party. Is it about the kiss?"

"No. Not at all." Her chin cocked up. She looked pissed, but she also looked hot. In that getup, with her perfectly smooth skin, her sexy dress, her meadow-green eyes. Hell, she even looked great wearing those wire-rimmed glasses. It suited her, and the beauty behind those glasses was unmistakable. "But if there's a next time, keep it to a minimum."

He sighed. "A minimum? You mean, don't make you moan?" he whispered.

She shot him a look that told him exactly what she thought of him.

"There will be more kisses, Gianna. Can't be

helped. Now, will you smile and pretend you're happy to be my fiancée?"

A few guests were heading in their general direction. She took note and plastered a big smile on her face. After they walked past, though, her smile faded. "How was that?" She batted her eyes like a 1920s movie star.

"It'll do, for starters."

Gianna put him on edge. She was mind-blowingly sexy and didn't even know it. But she was also a pain in his rear end. And he wasn't sure which of the two disturbed him more.

Gianna sat with Lily and Harper at one of the tables, while Gage picked up his guitar and joined his band onstage, treating the late-night die-hard guests to a song. There were fewer than forty people here now, many, she figured, who had waited around for this very thing. To hear Gage Tremaine sing. And he didn't disappoint. His voice was smooth, untarnished by time or repetition, the depth of his tone rich and sincere. He sang a beautiful ballad, aiming his blue-eyed attention not on the guests who sat mesmerized, but on her, as if there wasn't another soul at the party.

Opera and classical music were her preference, but she didn't doubt Gage's immense talent. And the words of the song, about love and loss and newfound hope, touched her deeply. He delivered the song as if he knew he could reach her with those lyrics, with the raw emotion he'd packed in them. As if he was singing of her grief and a future of promise.

Someone gently patted her hand, and she tore her gaze from Gage to look at his sister. "Are you okay?" Lily whispered.

Lily was astute enough to know this whole charade had been thrust upon her quickly and that she had a dozen puzzling thoughts roaming her mind at any one given moment. "I'm fine. It's a pretty song."

"But the way Gage kissed you—"

"It was just for show," she replied immediately.

Lily gave her head a little shake. "Really?" she asked softly. "Because it looked like both of you were into it, hot and heavy."

"That's what Gage wanted everyone to think," she offered.

"My brother's a good man, Gianna. But just be careful. A girl can get swept away by his charm and all the adulation surrounding him."

"Charm? Gage has charm?" She glanced at him again, his voice captivating the audience, making a liar out of her. "Don't worry. He doesn't affect me that way." ,

Lily didn't appear convinced, but she didn't argue the point.

After the song ended, Gage sang an upbeat tune, and everyone stood and moved along with the music. It was a fun, impromptu moment, and even she had to admit to enjoying herself.

The jam session went on for twenty more minutes, and as soon as Gage was through and the band members dispersed, the rest of the guests started to leave.

Several approached to wish them congratulations one more time on their way out.

Gianna's phone buzzed on the table. She picked it up and found a message from Brooke. "Excuse me," she told the rest of Gage's family. She walked over to a far, quiet corner of the yard and read the text.

Having a good time with my folks. Maine's amazing this time of year. Ben's here with Sadie and the kids. They loved the fireworks. How's your Fourth going? Anything delish to tell me? Gage?

The last time they'd spoken, Gianna had skirted the issue of Gage and what they were doing together at the ice cream shop and the Rhinestone Room. She wished she had the nerve to explain the "lie" in a way that Brooke would understand. Brooke worked at the university, too, as a counselor. They'd become great friends over the years, but they were more than that; they'd been each other's confidantes.

Glad you're having a great time. Miss you. Wish you were here tonight at the Tremaine estate. We need to talk.

What? She posted an upside-down emoji. Don't tell me you've fallen madly in love with Gage and your heart's all aflutter?

It was a tease. A joke. But never had Gianna felt the gravity of lying more than right now. She didn't want to do this to Brooke. She'd battled it over and over in her head until her brains were mush. And now her stomach ached in the worst way.

But she had to think on this logically. Because she was a logical kind of girl, right? If Gage hadn't told his band members the truth, guys he felt closest to, the fair thing for her to do was keep the charade going with Brooke.

She'd come to realize that nothing was really fair when the lie was this huge.

Actually, she typed in. Don't fall over, but Gage and I just got engaged. For real.

Her phone rang ten seconds later, and Gianna didn't have to look to know it was Brooke, ready to interrogate her.

She pushed the button to accept the call. "What? Tell me you're joking." Brooke's voice was elevated an octave. "Are you serious?"

She wished she wasn't. "I am serious. It's not a joke, Brooke. We fell in love and have kept it quiet out of reverence for my mother." She squeezed her eyes shut. She should be struck by lightning using that as an excuse.

Sorry, Mama.

"He is the exact opposite of you, Gia."

"I know. I guess it's true, opposites attract," she said. "We've known each other forever, Brooke."

"Maybe you only think you love him because of all the heartache you've been through lately."

"I don't think that's it, Brooke. I, uh, I really love him."

Her friend became very quiet. "And when were you going to tell me?"

"Tomorrow. Honestly, I'm still getting used to the idea myself. I'm sorry if you're hurt, Brooke. It's been a whirlwind."

"I'm not hurt. I only want you to be happy, Gianna. You've had a rough year, but I'm glad you told me tonight."

"Yes, me, too. Well, I'd better get back. I'll talk to you tomorrow, okay?"

"Okay…and congratulations, my friend. I…wish you all the best."

"Thanks. Love you."

"Same."

Ugh, that conversation had been grueling. Brooke still had reservations—she could tell by her skeptical tone. She knew Gianna too well. Brooke hadn't heard passion in her voice while she spoke of Gage. She hadn't heard excitement. Because there was none, and Gianna hadn't been all that convincing.

She tried not to blame Gage for getting her involved in this. But right now, her emotions were overriding her logic and good sense. You reap what you sow. Gage's occupation put his every move in the spotlight, and that very thing was what had caused all the trouble. Now she was a part of a sham that might make her lose Brooke's friendship if the lie was ever discovered, and she couldn't bear the thought of losing yet another person she loved.

By the time she returned, all the guests had gone. She found Gage by the stage, speaking with Cade and their mom. A crew was working cleanup, and servers were removing the last of the dishes and cutlery. Lily was over by the pool with Nathan, and if Gianna wasn't mistaken, the candles glistening on the water didn't twinkle half as much as Lily's eyes as she flirted coyly with the family's horse wrangler.

Gianna had a vivid imagination, but she wasn't imaging the way Nathan was looking at Lily, either, like she was a treasure of gold. Who could blame him? Lily was wonderful.

Gianna sighed and gathered her wits. She was in this thing now, for better or worse, and couldn't back out. She walked over to everyone. "Hi."

"Hello, dear," Rose said, giving her a little kiss on the cheek. "How are you holding up?"

She felt Gage's eyes on her. "I'm doing well. The party was really great. Harper, those fresh tarts you made were yummy."

"So was the five-layer American flag cake," Cade said, glancing at his soon-to-be wife. "I'm afraid you're stuck now, sweetheart. You're gonna have to make it every year from now on."

"Happy to."

"Yeah, I had two slices and would've gone in for thirds if given the chance," Gage said.

"Well, I think everyone had a nice time. And Gage, your announcement seemed to go over very well," Rose said.

"It'll be all over the news tomorrow. Trust me, I know," Harper said wryly. She'd been a reality star, who'd been disguised and in hiding when she'd met

Cade. He hadn't had a clue who she really was. But love conquered all, and the two were as happy as clams now.

"That was the point of all this, wasn't it? To make news?" Cade glanced at his brother. "Do me a favor, bro, don't invite any paparazzi to our wedding. We've had enough of that for three lifetimes."

"Oh, no. That's not going to happen," Gianna declared immediately. "We wouldn't dream of it. Some things are sacred. Your wedding certainly is."

"Damn," Gage said, as if just realizing reporters might try to crash the wedding. "I'll hire security to make sure of it. Nothing's gonna ruin your big day," he assured the couple.

"Well—" Rose placed her hand over her heart "—I certainly hope not."

"I promise, Mom." Gage kissed her cheek. "And thanks for allowing me to hijack the party tonight."

"I'm only glad my family was all here today." She took Gianna's hand. "My whole family."

Tears burned behind Gianna's eyes. She'd needed to hear that. Rose had always made her feel part of the family, but tonight especially, when she was feeling like such a fraud, Rose's love surrounded her and made her feel a bit better.

"I'm pretty tired. I think it's time I turn in." Rose kissed everyone good-night, and Cade and Harper escorted her into the house. Lily was off somewhere with Nathan, she supposed. Gianna hadn't seen her for quite some time now, which left just her and Gage standing in a yard that just a short time ago had been swarming with guests.

"Well, what do you say? Ready to turn in?" Gage asked.

She was beat. The physical toll didn't even begin to match the mental toll this day had taken on her. "My cheeks hurt from all the smiling I did tonight."

Gage reached for her hand, and she pretended not to notice as she turned and began walking toward the guesthouse. She wished to high heaven Gage wouldn't follow her. That he could find another place to sleep tonight. She needed privacy, but she doubted he'd agree, and quite honestly, she wasn't up for an argument.

Not tonight.

Not after that earth-shattering kiss.

Not on the evening of her fake engagement.

Five

Gianna tossed and turned in her bed. She couldn't sleep, the events of the entire day rehashing in her mind. She was living a lie and had to resign herself to the fact that for the next six weeks, she was at Gage's mercy. She'd been fine with that—*until he'd kissed her.* That kiss, powerful, masterful and filled with dire hunger, worried her no end. She was a red-blooded Italian girl who was passionate about her work, her students, her family. But she'd never experienced that kind of unbridled passion and desire for a man. And least of all Gage Tremaine.

"Until now," she whispered into the night.

She punched her pillow and tossed her head back again, squeezing her eyes shut. But it was no use. She knew in her bones that sleep would elude her right now. She might as well not waste her time wrestling with plaguing notions. She always had a ton of research waiting for her. She rose from bed and padded barefoot toward the kitchen, making doubly sure she was quiet as she passed Gage's bedroom.

Entering the kitchen, she filled an electric kettle with water. The pot heated water in twenty seconds flat, and she poured it into a teacup. Chamomile tea steeped, steam billowing up.

Movement caught her eye from the living room. She peeked out and found Gage sitting on the sofa, focused on a laptop, a whiskey glass in his hand. He was deep in thought and didn't seem to notice her. And then, as if he'd read her thoughts, he swiveled his head and spotted her.

Oh, man.

He rose, abandoning his computer. He took a quick sip of whiskey and sauntered over.

"Can't sleep?" he asked quietly.

She swallowed hard, forcing her gaze to his eyes and not on his bare, ultra-ripped chest. All he wore were faded blue jeans, the waistband dipping inches below his navel. There was a presence about him, an aura of sensual prowess causing her heart to pound.

"No, uh, just thought some tea would help."

He smiled and approached, keeping his eyes trained on her face and not the thigh-length white T-shirt she wore that screamed Fairmont U Tigers, complete with a menacing feline on the front. Her hair was up in a ridiculous bun, tousled from her fight with her pillows.

"Try this," he said, coming close and spilling some whiskey into her teacup.

"Gage, what are you doing?"

"Helping you get back to sleep. So I can get back to what I was doing."

"Am I disturbing you?"

He eyed her appearance, from her painted toenails to her legs, up her thighs, and then spending extra time perusing the tiger covering her breasts. She held her breath, wondering what he was thinking. Finally, his gaze roamed over her face to land on her silly hairdo. Hunger flashed in his eyes, and he sipped whiskey again.

"No."

"I'm glad. What are you doing up at this hour?"

"When I can't sleep, I get up and write."

"Write?"

"Songs. Well, the lyrics to music. Didn't think you'd appreciate me fiddling with my guitar this late at night."

"That was probably wise, though I'm up now anyway."

"Sip your tea. It'll knock you out."

"Because I'm a lightweight?"

"Absolutely." He smiled and finished off his drink. "And because I make you nervous."

She set her teacup down, her hands shaking. "What are you talking about?"

"Nothing. Forget I said anything."

"You do not make me nervous, Gage Tremaine."

"I don't? You liked that kiss as much as I did. Admit it."

She folded her arms across her T-shirt, which brought his gaze to her chest again. "I will not admit anything. Besides, it was all for show."

"Yeah, all for show," he repeated, folding his arms across his chest now, too, taking a stance. "But what if it wasn't?"

"I don't deal in what-ifs, Gage."

"I'm just saying, what if that kiss wasn't a fluke? *What if* it's the best kiss either one of us have ever had? *What if* we try it again, just to be sure?"

"You want to kiss me again? Right here and now. Without an audience?" She backed up a step, picked up her teacup and sipped, needing the fortification. The whiskey burned her throat going down, and her eyes opened wide. "No, thanks."

"Nervous?"

"Gage, you can't be serious? Look at us, the way we're dressed, or rather, undressed." She scanned his body again, the muscles in his arms and bare chest so glorious her insides heated up. He was positively beautiful in the flesh.

"I'm looking. And I like what I see."

"Me? I'm a mess. Don't even go there, Gage."

"You don't even know how tempting you are."

She rubbed her forehead. "This is crazy." Then she glared at him. "Are you trying to make me crazy?"

"No."

She grabbed her teacup and walked past him. "Well, you are. So cut it out. I'm going to bed."

"I don't suppose that's an invitation."

She turned to him, suddenly imagining him in her bed. Imagining more kisses like the one tonight. She imagined touching him in all his hard places, and her hesitation caused his brows to rise with hope.

She was just a convenience to him, a woman who was handy and who would be spending the next month with him. She wasn't a superfan, wasn't interested in him. She didn't even like him that much. "Have another drink, Gage. *What if* we forget this conversation ever happened?"

"Sure, I'm good at pretending."

"I know that about you. That's why I'm going to bed now. Alone."

He grinned. "Don't worry. You don't have to lock your door. That's not my style."

The man was impossible. Impossibly sexy. Impossibly confident. But he was right. He didn't have to force a situation. Gage didn't have to work too hard to get women to fall at his feet.

She just had to make sure she wasn't one of those women.

For the next few days, Gianna's phone rang more than it had the entire year. Suddenly she was sought after. People she hadn't heard from in a long time began calling. Her high school friends, her old roommates, people who hadn't come to her mother's funeral all of a sudden were leaving her messages of congratulations. She was the woman who'd captured

Gage Tremaine's heart, and now she was deemed worthy of their attention.

Her engagement to the country superstar had made headline news, and Gage's phone was also ringing off the hook. He was scheduled for morning shows, late-night talk shows and a few music events.

People were curious about their relationship, about their almost minuscule courtship. How had Gage hidden Gianna in plain sight, they wanted to know. When did he fall in love with her, exactly, was the question of the day. Gianna's professional record had been scrutinized pretty thoroughly. They'd reported on her college days and on how she'd come to work at Fairmont U. They'd written about her various awards and accomplishments. Most of what they wrote was complimentary, as if the press and Gage's music colleagues had put their stamp of approval on their engagement.

Tremaine's Engagement Sets off Fireworks.

Gage and the Professor, a Match Made in Country Heaven?

Professor Gives Tremaine an A Grade.

And just like that, Gianna was thrust into Gage's world. Luckily, Gage had left her alone most of the time, allowing her to do her research. She didn't know where he went during the day, but they'd always meet up at the main house for dinner with his family. And in the evenings, he'd walk her back to the guesthouse and wish her good-night.

She relished the peace and quiet, but all that was about to change this morning. She had packed last night for their trip to Nashville, and they were flying out soon.

She was dressed in new jeans and a pink chiffon blouse with bell sleeves. Another one of Lily's picks. A matching jacket would work well when on the plane, she'd said. With Gage's approval, Lily had taken one of his credit cards one day and gone on a shopping spree, coming back with a dozen new outfits for Gianna's travels.

The toaster popped up her bread nice and crispy, and as she spread butter on it, Gage walked into the kitchen, dressed casually, too, his phone to his ear.

"Yeah, okay, Regan," he said, giving Gianna a quick good-morning smile. "We'll be there on time. Gianna, too. I know, I know. We'll talk later."

She poured them both a cup of coffee and sat down at the table. Gage shut off his phone and took a seat facing her. Why did he always look so good in the morning? His hair had yet to be combed. Even tousled, it looked amazing. And the morning scruff darkening his face was heavier than usual today, making him look even *sexier*, if that were possible.

"Thanks for the coffee," he said, running a hand through his hair. The more unruly, the better, it seemed.

"You're welcome." They'd found a certain rhythm together these past few days. Gage had been on his best behavior around her lately, and that made her wary.

He took a sip and sighed. "This is good."

"Problems?" She'd gotten to know his moods, and this one today wasn't good.

"Why do you ask?"

"There's a face you make when you're irritated about something."

"You know my faces?"

"Mostly your sour ones. Remember what I do for a living, Gage. I study emotions and relationships."

"I'll keep that in mind."

"So what's up? And if it's none of my business, I'm sure you'll tell me."

"Unfortunately, it does involve you. And I want you to keep an open mind."

She didn't like the sound of this. "Why? What now?" she asked.

"Well, uh." He sucked in a deep breath, as if he'd rather have a root canal on both sides of his mouth than tell her. "It seems as if our engagement news is bigger than we expected. Regan booked us on *The Johnny O in the Morning* show. It's the hottest ticket on the air in the South, and well, they want to interview both of us."

"Us? As in you and me?" He couldn't be serious. She wasn't supposed to be the story, he was. She was to be his trophy fiancée, showing up at events, but certainly not being a part of them. She didn't sign up for this. "I'm not doing it, Gage."

"Regan said it's important. We did such a good job of convincing the world we're in love that now the public wants to see us together."

"They've got lots of photos of us, Gage. Isn't that enough?"

"Apparently not. Look, I told Regan not to involve you, but she says it's too good an opportunity to pass up. They want us for tomorrow morning. And if you don't show, it's a deal breaker."

She bit her lip, shaking her head. It was a lot to ask of her. "Gage, I don't want to do this."

"All right, I guess I'll call Regan back and tell her to forget it. I suppose it's not the end of the world."

He was surprisingly gracious about it, which made her feel like a heel.

In her heart, she didn't want to sacrifice what little privacy she had left, but her darn analytical brain told her the whole purpose for this ruse was to enhance and revive Gage's image. "If you cancel the interview, that sorta defeats the purpose of this charade, doesn't it? I'm doing this to help boost your image, not to turn down ideal opportunities."

Hope entered his eyes. "Are you changing your mind?"

"I'm looking at it logically. It makes sense. The sooner you fix your reputation, the sooner this whole thing will be over."

"So?" His brows rose, and hope, again, registered on his face. *Like a little boy getting his wish.*

"So…you're gonna owe me for this."

"Ha! You mean more than I already owe you? I would be more than grateful, Gianna. You'd have me over a barrel. Not too many wo—uh, people can say that."

"Gage, you know how much I hate being the center of attention."

"I do know."

"We're opposites in most every way."

"I know that, too. But if anyone can pull off a convincing interview, it would be you. You're a smart cookie."

Was she? Would a smart cookie get herself into this situation in the first place? "I think that's a compliment."

"It is," he said without hesitation.

Gianna squeezed her eyes shut. She knew she had no choice. Regan was right—this was too good an opportunity to squander. And it would get them to the finish line that much sooner. She sighed and looked deep into his eyes. "I might regret it, but I'll do it. Just. This. One. Time."

Gage immediately grinned. He rose, pulling her up from her chair and wrapping both his arms around her in an enormous hug. Her nose went to his neck, and she breathed in his fresh, soapy scent, felt the power of his ripped chest against her breasts, the warmth of his body pulsing around her. "Thank you." He pressed a kiss to her cheek before releasing her.

They stared at each other, a few moments ticking by. Did that demonstrative hug rattle him as much as it did her? She couldn't tell, but she did know one thing—making Gage happy could very well be infectious.

Gage was first to break the silence. "Well, I'll just go get our luggage. Are you all packed?"

"Pretty much."

"The limo will be here in thirty minutes."

"I'll be ready."

But was she ready to spend time with Gage on the road? Spend her nights with him in a hotel room? Pretend that she was madly in love with him while on television?

She sighed. For a woman who kept things simple, her life was getting more and more complicated.

The chartered plane had amenities galore, from luxurious seats and tables to a couch for relaxing and enough food to feed the Fairmont Tigers football team. Gage didn't think much of it. He was accustomed to traveling this way, but for her, a girl with middle-class values, it all seemed over the top.

"The price of fame," Gage had said when they'd first boarded. He wasn't being sarcastic, either. He explained that he couldn't take commercial airlines anymore. It wasn't worth the scrutiny and the constant attention. Folks in other parts of the country weren't as thoughtful as in his hometown in Juliet County.

The trip lasted a little more than an hour, and when they touched down in Nashville, a certain thrill ran up and down her spine. There was so much history here. The town rivaled New Orleans in terms of history, music and excitement.

Gianna's eyes were wide-open as they traveled the streets, taking in the sights, the incredible landscapes. And when they pulled up to the Gaylord Opryland

Resort, she was immediately struck by the grandeur and opulence of this fabulous hotel.

A doorman opened their limo door. "Welcome to the Gaylord," he said. Gage unfolded his body to a standing position and then reached for her hand. "Here we are," he said.

Gianna stepped out of the limo and was immediately struck by a blast of humidity. In the South, one could always count on drippy, cling-to-your-body kind of heat in summer. Gianna was used to it. She once spent three days without air-conditioning in her university classroom when the air reached 90 percent humidity. Nashville was no different, it seemed.

But as they approached the entrance, hand in hand, a blast of cool air welcomed them. She stood by Gage's side in the lobby as he checked in, keeping her gaze focused on him and not the dozen pairs of knowing eyes on the country music star.

Ten minutes later, they were in their hotel suite, Gage keeping to his promise of two-bedroom accommodations. She strolled out to the balcony to view cascading waterfalls in a lush green setting. There were waterways and bridges within the interior perimeter of the hotel, brightened by the sun's rays streaming down from the massive overhead skylight.

Gage joined her on the balcony, handing her a glass of ice-cold water. "It's really magnificent."

"It is," he said, leaning against the wrought iron railing. "I love coming here."

"How many times have you sung at the Opry?" she asked. She'd never been, but everyone knew that singing at the Grand Ole Opry meant you'd hit your career high mark.

"About five times, I'd say. Never gets old."

"No. I guess not."

"So, now that we're here, what's next?" she asked.

"We relax for a bit. Then I'll take you anywhere you want to go."

She smiled. "Really?"

He nodded. "Remember, I owe you."

"I'd love to see some of the city, but shouldn't we go over what I'm going to say at tomorrow's interview?" Her stomach churned just thinking about it. "I mean, I need to know essentials about you, don't I?"

He shot her a glib smile. "I don't think anyone's going to ask you what my favorite color is. Or what I eat for breakfast. Or how many awards I've won."

She hesitated, blinking rapidly. She didn't know any of those things.

"Six, in case you were wondering."

"Six? I had no idea. I'm glad you told me. Who was your last girlfriend?" she asked. "Just because I don't want to be ignorant of your past."

"I haven't dated much. That incident with Bobette Jones sort of destroyed my trust."

"She was the one who claimed you were cheating on her?"

"We'd broken up quietly just a month before, and no one knew. So, when she found out I had a date, *one* date, with another woman, she went to the press and claimed I cheated on her. It was probably the nicest thing she told them about me that day. Hell, one woman is more than enough for me to figure out, much less trying to maneuver two at the same time. But I got the blame. She painted a picture of me as a cheating jerk, just to get back at me."

"Hell hath no fury like a woman scorned."

"Yeah. None of it was true, but then couple that with the other two unfortunate situations I had, and suddenly I'm viewed as some sort of heartbreaker bad boy."

"What she did to you wasn't fair, Gage. I'm sorry. I never knew the entire story. At least now, if I'm asked about it, I can say something in your defense."

His brows arched, and gratitude filled his eyes. "You'd do that?"

She nodded. She didn't want him to get the wrong idea. "Of course. Any fiancée would do that same."

"You'd stand by your man?" He spoke softly, his blue eyes twinkling. And his smile was real—he wasn't teasing her.

"Yeah, that's why I'm here, isn't it? I legitimize you."

He winced, his twinkle gone now. She'd been blunt, but it wasn't anything they hadn't discussed before. "I suppose so."

Gage turned away, looking out onto the view before him. "We've been spotted," he said, gesturing to a group of news reporters on the ground level, and just like that, his hand covered hers and she was being drawn up against his chest. "Legitimize me right now," he whispered, his gaze sharp and penetrating.

"Do you mean…?"

He nodded. "Yes, I mean kiss me."

But he didn't wait—he bent his head and instantly covered her mouth. She was stunned into silence, just like the last time. And while he was putting on a good show, her stomach flipped over itself from his performance. His arms came around her waist and their hips collided. She fought against the urge to moan, to whimper as he drove his tongue into the recesses of her mouth. The invasion was surprisingly welcome. Gage took her on a masterful journey, giving and taking, and then giving again.

Everything below her waist melted. Gage had the opposite dilemma. He was granite-hard, and it was both exhilarating and a little frightening how quickly he could turn on. How quickly *he could turn her on*.

By the time he ended the kiss, she could barely breathe. Gage wasn't doing much better. His chest pumped up and down as he pulled away.

She grabbed the collar of his shirt and gazed adoringly into his eyes. "Well, we showed them, didn't we?" Maybe too well.

He gazed right back at her, catching his breath. "We…did. You're a quick study."

But was it really necessary to put on such a display? She wasn't sure.

He turned his back on the balcony railing and tugged her into the suite, closing the double doors behind him. To all, it looked as if they were heading to the bedroom.

At least, that's what a real couple would do. But

they were far from that. "I think I'll unpack and get some rest."

Gage rubbed the back of his neck, hesitating a moment, as if he was going to say something. Then he just nodded and watched her walk away.

"Do you always lose track of time that way when you're working?" Gage asked, sipping red wine as they sat down to dinner at the hotel's outdoor steak house. The soothing rush of the waterfall and soft music playing in the background gave the restaurant a relaxing ambience.

"Most times I do. I swear I was just checking some stats, and then the next thing I know, I'm knee-deep in research." She pushed her glasses up her nose. "The time flew by." They'd never made it outside the hotel today. "I apologize."

"I thought you were napping all that time. Or, worse yet, that you were running scared after we kissed."

"You were wrong on both counts." Gianna sipped her wine. This time she'd stick to half a glass. She had to be on her toes around Gage. He had wild kissing skills.

"So what were you researching that fascinated you so much?" he asked. He'd changed for dinner and looked nice in a snap-down tan shirt and black jeans. His dark hair, touching his collar, was as long as she'd ever seen it. He epitomized a handsome-as-the-devil country rock star. "Divorce rates."

He nearly choked on his merlot. "Divorce rates,"

he repeated, coming forward in his seat. "I can see how that can keep you awake all afternoon."

Her mouth twitched. Gage was such a tease.

"Tell me something interesting about divorce rates."

She didn't hesitate. "Well, did you know that over thirty percent of divorces occur when the woman feels the man doesn't take her career seriously?"

"Thirty percent, huh? And what's the other seventy percent caused by?"

"Oh, that's from having men overrate their kissing abilities."

Gianna lifted her glass and smiled at Gage.

He burst out laughing. "You really had me going there for a minute."

"I know. And I also know that you think my research isn't valuable. But I assure you it is."

"I never once said anything of the kind."

"You have selective memory. You've teased me about my work hundreds of times."

Gage shook his head. "Teasing doesn't count. It's just what I do, with you."

She smiled because she knew there were eyes on her. She was coming to realize that no matter where they went, people were going to recognize Gage Tremaine. Especially in Nashville, Tennessee.

"So tell me, if you could go anywhere in the world, where would you want to go?" he asked.

"Why are you asking me that?"

"We should keep the conversation going, since we're being watched." He sipped again, swirling wine in the glass. "And I'm curious about what places fascinate you."

"Europe. Brooke and I had a trip planned a year ago. Specifically to visit Italy and Greece. My heritage. I'm one-quarter Greek, too. We were really looking forward to going. It was one of the things on my bucket list. Only, life interfered when Mama got so sick."

"You'll get there one day, Gianna."

"Maybe." She wasn't thinking that far into the future right now. She had to get through one day at a time now.

"Would you like to take a drive with me after dinner?" he asked.

"Where'd you have in mind?"

His mouth quirked up. "The place where I cut my musical teeth."

She tilted her head, giving it some thought. Gage could be charming when he set out to be. And after that kiss, with all the sizzling-hot stirrings it created, she should refuse. She had the perfect excuse. "I do have more research to do." Allotting her plenty of work time was part of the deal they'd agreed to. Going out with him when not absolutely necessary wasn't.

"It's a place you should see. For the interview. You can say it was the first place I took you to in Nashville. And that wouldn't be a lie."

"No, I guess it wouldn't. Is it fancy? Should I change my clothes?" She was wearing a floral summer dress with spaghetti straps, her hair down around her shoulders.

"No need to change. You might be overdressed for the honky-tonk I'm taking you to, but you sure do look pretty tonight."

Heat rushed up her neck. "Thank you."

An hour later, Gage held her hand as they walked down Broadway, the street bustling with tourists and musicians, Nashville nightlife in full swing. "This is the place where dreams are made. Or hearts are broken. I know some guys, and ladies alike, who've spent years trying to get their big break here."

"It does remind me of New Orleans. There's so much energy here."

"That's a good way to put it."

"So how did you get your big break?"

They strolled the sidewalk, country twang, laughter and conversation pouring out of the bars as they walked along. Several people recognized Gage and stopped to take a picture of him. It didn't faze him much that he had no privacy, but it wasn't a life Gianna could ever get used to.

"Me? I was in a band in college, and on a dare, we came to Nashville. But there were no gigs for amateurs like us. I mean, we were really raw, but we loved making music. I never expected to make a living at it. My path was always to help my family with the business.

"One day, me and the guys sauntered into Lucky Red's Bar to get a beer, and it turned out, the band they had booked was involved in a car accident. None of them were seriously injured, but they couldn't get to Lucky's in time. I guess you could say what was bad luck for them was my lucky break. I wound up singing two sets that night. We did so well, we got booked for the next month. And then one day Regan Fitzgerald walked into Lucky's scouting new talent, and the rest is history."

"Wow, I find it amazing that your career was left to chance like that. I mean, up until that point, you had no idea if you were going to make it as a musician."

"It's the nature of the beast, I guess. It's a well-known fact that some of the best talent in the country—singers, guitarists, drummers—are pining away in some local honky-tonk. Or playing a lounge act in Vegas. Like I said, some hearts get broken."

"Tough. I couldn't do it. I couldn't leave my future to chance like that. I always knew what I wanted to do with my life."

"And you made that happen. You worked hard for your success."

"Because I knew it was achievable."

"Where's the challenge in that?" He grinned.

She swatted at his arm. "You're impossible."

Gage grabbed her hand and immediately brought her in, looking deep into her eyes. He had a way of cradling her body as if she was something precious, something he didn't want to let go. He tipped his hat lower on his forehead. "We're being watched."

"I know."

He gestured toward the bar in front of them. Lucky Red's. "Want to go inside?"

"It's why we came."

"Always so logical."

Their hands entwined, he led her into the bar. A band was up on the tiniest stage in the back, with just enough room for three musicians and the lead singer. The place was jam-packed, couples dancing on the floor, servers nearly spilling topped-off beers, the music more country rock than twang and loud enough to bust eardrums.

"Want a drink?" he asked, heading over to the bar.

"Sure, I'll take a beer."

He gave her a look. "Beer?"

"Sure, I like beer." Occasionally, she'd have a beer. And she wanted to look like she fit in. "Make that a light beer. And no jokes about me being a light-weight."

"No jokes," he promised and called over to the bartender. The man turned, recognition registering on his face. "Hey, Gage. Good to see you."

"Hey, Red. Same here."

The two men shook hands over the bar. "It's been quite some time, boy. You back to cause a ruckus?"

Gage grinned. "Never in here, Red. I came to show my fiancée, Gianna, the place. She's never been to Nashville. Thought she'd want to see where it all started. Gianna, honey, this ole guy is Red Muldoon. He's owned this honky-tonk going on forty years."

"That's right. Opened the place on New Year's Eve 1982. Nice to meet you, miss. And congratulations. Won't pretend I don't know about your engagement. Been big news around here, you know."

"Yes, I suppose it has," she replied. "Nice to meet you, too, Mr. Muldoon."

The man's mouth twisted up. "It's Red. Just plain ole Red."

She found the whiskered man endearing and immediately liked him. "Okay, Red. It's a great place you have here."

"I appreciate it." He turned to the other barkeep. "Get these two anything they want. On the house."

"Yes, sir." The starstruck young man behind the bar nodded.

"That's not necessary, Red."

"You know your money's not good here. But I wouldn't kick you in the shin if you wanted to give the crowd a taste of your music."

"Will do," Gage said, tipping his hat. "A little later."

"Whenever you're ready. Tell Ronny what you're having and we'll get it to you pronto."

Their attention was brought to the singer onstage crooning a love song, one so poignant the noisy patrons all simmered down to listen.

"He's good, but he's no Gage Tremaine." Red slapped Gage on the back. "Now, go dance with your lady. I'll get a table cleaned up for you both."

"Sounds good."

Red walked off, and Gage ordered their drinks at the bar, giving the guy a huge tip before turning to her. "Want to legitimize me some more?" he asked.

Before Gianna could open her mouth to refuse, her hand was entwined with his and she was led to the dance floor.

"What are you doing?"

"Dancing with my lady." Gage winked playfully. "The crowd expects it."

Gage dragged her to his chest so quickly, air whooshed out of her lungs. His arms were like anchors around her waist, keeping her close. Her heart began to dance, far sooner than her body moved.

Goodness, they were the focus of attention again. This time, she didn't have to look around. She sensed eyes on both of them. "Do you always do what the crowd wants?" she whispered. A hint of his cologne invaded her nostrils, the scent wildly erotic.

"Actually," he whispered back, "I'm at my very best when there isn't a crowd. When it's just one on one."

Goose bumps rose up her arms. Gage liked to keep her close, but the contact battled with her good senses. She couldn't pull away. Others on the dance floor were watching intently, waiting.

A good defense is a powerful offense, and she was learning quickly that she needed to take the helm. "Conceited, aren't you?"

Her jab didn't even faze him. "Nope. Just solid fact."

His confidence stunned her. She gave her head a shake. "Amazing."

"That's what they tell me."

But his boast didn't really bother her, not in the way it should. He had provoked her curiosity about his prowess, about what it would be like to make love with him. To be the object of his desire and have the full force of his sexual attention aimed at her. For real.

She hadn't had a satisfying sexual experience in… well, maybe never. The few men she'd been with didn't exactly make the earth quake.

And there was no doubt, as much as she hated to admit it to herself, Gage Tremaine was…*delicious*. Sexually speaking.

"Put your head on my shoulder," he whispered as the music played on.

"Why?"

"Because for some reason you're scowling."

Oh!

She pressed her head to his chest. The pounding of his heart reverberated in her ears. She shouldn't be surprised by the tight contact. They'd danced this way before. At the Fourth of July bash, when they'd lied to the world about being in love.

"That's better," he said into her ear. "What's with the sour face?"

"Nothing." Except images flashed in her head of getting bare-butt naked with him. It really freaked her out.

"You hate this, don't you?"

She did. She really did. Lusting for her fake fiancée wasn't in the plan. And wouldn't Gage just have a big laugh over it if he ever found out?

"It's not so bad, Gage," she lied. She couldn't let him guess her wanton thoughts. That, if things were different, she'd jump his bones. "I can live with it. For a little while longer."

At the table, after they guzzled beer—well, Gage did all the guzzling, Gianna merely sipped—Red brought over three decadent desserts. Red had a sweet tooth, and his honky-tonk was known for serving a variety of amazing treats. Gianna sampled chocolate surprise, a mound of chocolate infused with warm raspberry sauce. A person could gain three pounds just by looking at it. Gage tried the apple cobbler deluxe, with almonds, walnuts and cashews on top. And they both indulged in a bite of warm cookie pie, the dessert too rich to have more than one bite.

Gianna leaned way back in her chair and rubbed her tummy. "I'm gonna bust right out of this dress if I take one more bite."

Gage's brows rose. "I'd pay good money to see it."

"Funny, Gage."

His eyes shadowed. A deep sigh escaped his throat. Was he imagining her minus her dress? "Is it?"

Okay, maybe not so funny. Awareness struck like a match whenever he teased her this way. She blamed it on the smoky surroundings, the hum of the crowd, the sultry ballad the singer crooned. She wouldn't fall victim to it, to him. She had to remember why she was doing this. She had to remember another man with charm to spare. Another man, like Gage, who'd broken hearts. "Yes, it's ridiculous."

Not a minute later, Red called attention to Gage from the stage. "Everybody, in case you didn't notice, we've got our own Gage Tremaine in the house. And if you're inclined, I think he'll come up here to sing for us."

Whistles and shouts broke out, and the place erupted in applause. Gage rose from his seat, in the limelight once again. But that wasn't enough for him. *Oh, no.* "Come with me," he said, extending his hand.

"What? No," she blurted out quietly. "They don't want to see me."

"Not true. They want to see us. Together." He winked. "C'mon."

Given little choice, she put her hand in his and followed in his footsteps. The crowd parted, some slapping Gage on the back, others happy to eye him or take cell-phone photos. And once they stepped onstage, he held on tight, keeping one arm around her waist.

He said a few words to the band and turned, facing the crowd from behind the mic. "Thanks for the warm welcome," he said. "I appreciate the support. Truth is, I haven't sung in public since a broken beer bottle flew into my neck and slashed my throat. Yeah, that was unfortunate. Some of you might have heard a little something about that."

Chuckles rang out. Gage could be charming when he had to be.

"But then," he said, turning his blue-eyed gaze on her, "I wouldn't have met up with this pretty lady again. Everyone, I'm proud to have you meet Miss Gianna Marino. My fiancée."

Cheers went up, and Gianna smiled and waved.

"And yes, folks, she is a professor and one smart lady." He winked at her again. "'Cause she's marrying me."

The patrons ate it up. Gage was a good actor. The very best.

He took up the mic and sang to her, a fun song about fishing and baseball. Everyone in the place knew the words and sang to their hearts' content.

The music was contagious, the song so full of joy that she moved along with the crowd, clapping her hands, tapping her feet. The song ended, and a band member handed Gage a guitar. He grabbed two bar stools and gestured for her to take a seat.

Darn, the entire crowd watched her lumber up onto it. Grace not her strong suit, she managed to finally make herself comfortable on the thing.

Gage strummed a few notes, and the room quieted. He began to sing again, this time a soulful ballad, a love song that caressed the ears, a sweepingly beautiful tune about finding love for the very first time. Gage kept his eyes on her, and she forced herself to keep her gaze steady on him, but as the song went on, moving her, stroking her and touching her in ways she couldn't logically explain, she was captured by his deep, rich tone and his beautiful blue eyes.

It was a rare moment, to be caught up so fully in one man.

When the song ended, Gianna gazed out to the audience. Many starry-eyed women stared at her, envy in their eyes. A battalion of goose bumps rose up her arms. Was Gage getting to her? Was she falling victim to his charisma, his charm?

Gage's mouth lifted, satisfaction written on his face. He cupped her neck, drew her close and pressed a solid kiss to her lips.

Wow. Really, wow. Her heart sped wildly.

Was she a gooey-eyed woman now, too, mesmerized by a compelling voice and deadly good looks? Wasn't that Gage's intent? To convince people they were madly in love? And judging by the applause breaking out, it was working.

"Thank you, folks. But I'm afraid I have to say good-night now. It's time for me to take my lady home."

Her feminist side should be up in arms. She wasn't anyone's lady, but Gage's tone indicated something far different. He was hers and she was his, in a way that delighted both women and men alike. Gage obviously knew how to enchant the crowd. And confuse the heck out of her.

She was coming to her senses after his *display*. And she wasn't happy.

He led her offstage, both waving, Gage also tipping his hat. They stopped by the bar and found the owner vigorously wiping down the countertop.

"Good night, Red," Gage said. "Nice seeing you again." The men shook hands.

"Same. You're always welcome here. And don't forget me when you're handing out wedding invites."

Gage put his hand to his heart. "You got it."

"Nice meeting you, miss."

"Thanks for your hospitality." He really was a lovable, kind of rough-around-the-edges ole guy.

"As I said, anytime." He gave her a wink.

They stepped outside, and her shoulders dropped down. Tension oozed out of her. She'd been put on display and that wasn't something she enjoyed. Gage reached for her hand, and instead of giving it to him, she fidgeted with the straps of her purse. She needed breathing room from him. All his touching and kissing was confusing her. He'd warned her they'd have to show affection, but there'd been no clear warning she'd actually respond to it—to him. And enjoy it.

She strode quietly down the street, picking up the pace, getting a few steps away from him. *Breathing room.*

He caught up in just a few strides. "Hey, what's wrong?" he asked.

"Nothing," she snapped. "Thanks for introducing me to Red. But the show's over now. And I'm super tired."

"*Cranky* is a better word."

"Okay, so I'm cranky. Sue me."

"Wow." Noisy air pushed out of his chest. "You're not kiddin'."

"No, I'm not kidding. Are you forgetting about the interview tomorrow? I'm going to have to do this all over again."

"Didn't seem like you minded all that very much. You were getting all moony-eyed and sweet on me."

"I was not sweet on you." She wasn't going to go there with him. "Do you like lying to your friend?"

"No, I…uh. Actually, I don't. But it's a white lie. Not meant to hurt anybody."

"A lie is a lie, Gage."

"Well, then." He crossed his arms over his chest and leaned back on his boot heels. "Why don't you quit lying to yourself?"

Her eyes squeezed shut. "I don't lie to myself."

"You like it when I kiss you."

"Geesh, Gage." She would admit no such thing. Even if it was a little bit true. It would serve no purpose to swell his ego that way. "Don't be ridiculous."

"Okay…but just so you know, for me, kissing you is the very best thing that's come out of this charade. And I'm not *lying*."

"TMI, Gage." The frustrated woman in her wanted to cover her ears. "I don't want to hear it."

She hastened her steps, leaving him in the dust, and this time, he didn't try to catch up.

Six

He rode in the back of the limo, Gianna in the seat beside him, on the way to the television station. The morning show started at 8:00 a.m., and they were just about to arrive. As quiet as a mouse, Gianna sat staring at notes on her tablet. He had no doubt she would deliver. She was smart, sharp and didn't give an inch. Maybe she wore her conservative clothes this morning, a beige dress and matching blazer, to remind herself of who she really was, Professor Gianna Marino, and not some smitten fangirl who'd captured his heart. Her dark hair was up, as tight as her expression, and her shoes were sensible heels.

But she couldn't fool him. They had chemistry; whether it was convenient or not, it was there. No sense denying it. She wasn't faking her response to his kisses. Electricity filled the air when they were in the same room, or the same car. Was it her resistance to him that intrigued him most about her? Was it the challenge she posed? Or the fact that she was forbidden fruit?

His mother's warning came to mind.

Gianna's vulnerable. Don't take advantage of her.

His promises had seemed easy to keep at the time. Now, not so much.

The limo stopped in front of the WKN building, and the driver opened Gianna's door. Her head up, she exited the limo, taking the chauffeur's helpful hand. Gage got out right after her and immediately entwined their fingers, forming a united front. "Are you ready for this?"

"I always study for an exam."

"Good." The lady came prepared. Gage was more the fly-by-the-seat-of-your-pants kind of guy. That's why he sang for a living and she was an intellect.

"It's normal to be nervous," he assured her. Even though her smile was wide, the expression in her pretty green eyes wavered. "Took me quite a few before I got comfortable answering questions on live TV."

"Then I'm *very* normal. And this is the one and only one, Gage."

"I know. I appreciate it."

Half an hour later, he and Gianna sat on a couch facing Johnny O'Flannery on the live stage. Gage kept his arm around Gianna's shoulder, partly for show, but mostly to give her support. Hell, he'd practically forced her into doing this.

"Welcome back," the host said after the commercial break. "And we have a real treat for you this morning. We're joined by country superstar Gage Tremaine and his lovely brand-new fiancée, Professor Gianna Marino. Hi, you two."

"Good to see you, Johnny," Gage said.

"Nice to be here." Gianna smiled at the famous host.

"Well, can I start out by saying you two make a great couple?"

"Thanks." Gage tightened his hold on Gianna, bringing her shoulders closer to him.

"Gianna, congratulations on your engagement. It came as quite a surprise. Where has Gage been hiding you all this time? Is there any news you want to share with our viewers?"

"News?" Gianna said. "I think I can end the speculation right now. We're not ready to start a family just yet. We want to spend time together first as a married couple." Gianna shot him a warm, loving glance. "One day, maybe. Right, sweetheart?"

Gage cleared his throat. He wasn't prepared for that question right out of the gate. But there must've been some speculation that he'd gotten Gianna pregnant and that was the reason for the quick engagement. Little did they know, aside from a few kisses, he hadn't touched Gianna that way. Yet, man oh man, lately, he'd been imagining it. "Yeah, of course we want kids. But we want to enjoy some time alone.

Gianna and I have just reconnected. I want her all to myself first for a little bit."

"Gianna, you've known Gage most of your life. Why now, people are asking?" Johnny asked.

She sat up straighter and leaned forward slightly. Her body language skills were top-notch. "Yes, that's right. Our families are close. Gage and I tiptoed around each other for years, but when he was injured recently in an unfortunate brawl, I realized my true feelings for him. I guess you could say it was mutual, and long overdue. And we didn't have to take time to get to know one another like other couples do." Gianna set her warm, sweet gaze on him. "So our love came naturally, growing over the years."

Gianna spoke with such conviction, her words hitting home, and his heart lurched. He almost believed her, and it didn't scare him or make him flinch. Instead, warmth spread through him like golden honey. Gage took her hand and lifted it to his lips. Her skin was so dang soft, her hand delicate in his, and every time he touched her in any way, even under camera lights, his heart bumped into high gear. He placed a kiss on her hand. Oohs and aahs rang out in the studio audience.

"And very long overdue," he added.

"Gianna, would you say opposites attract? A university professor, who, I heard, doesn't even like country music, marrying a bad boy superstar?"

A sweet smile graced Gianna's expression. "Perhaps they do. But Gage is far from a bad person. I stand behind him completely and believe in his innocence. I have faith in him, in us. And I'm gaining a fine appreciation for country music now. Gage's voice, in my opinion, is unequaled. He's got a gift."

"Can't argue with that," Johnny replied. "But his fans might disagree about his back-to-back scandals lately."

"They're smart people. They know the real Gage Tremaine. He's not a cheater. He's a true gentleman. His fans know that."

Lately, he'd had a series of unfortunate incidents. He couldn't figure his string of bad luck. Sometimes, fame and fortune wasn't all it was cracked up to be. But now he was fighting back, Gianna helping him in his quest.

"So tell us a few things about yourself, Professor," Johnny asked. "The entertainment world wants to get to know you better."

"Well, I was raised by a loving single mother, Tonette Marino," she began. "My father...uh, my father's been gone a long while. Life wasn't always easy for the two of us, but I knew I had Mama's support no matter what I tried to accomplish. I was a scholarship student and achieved my professorship three years ago. I teach communication and family relationships, and my pet project is Learning and Literacy, a special foundation for children. We're always looking for volunteers and donations, for those of your viewers who may be interested in lending a helping hand."

"Is that what inspires you?"

"Everything about learning inspires me, but children who struggle to read are at a great disadvantage."

"I have to say I'm impressed by your dedication. But this must be a difficult time for you. Your mother passed away recently."

Gianna put her head down.

"It's still painful for her," Gage interjected, "so we don't talk about it in public." Gianna shouldn't have to speak about her grief. Some things needed to stay private.

"No, it's okay, sweetheart." Gianna focused on the host, her eyes a little watery. "He's always trying to protect me. Let's just say I miss my mother every second of the day."

"Terribly sorry for your loss, Gianna." Johnny's eyes softened.

Hearing her put it that way softened him up, too. Gianna was in pain every damn day. She wasn't a wilting flower about it, though. She'd done a good job of convincing the world they were a match made in heaven. Hell, he'd even interrupted the interviewer to protect her, and while she might've thought that was all for show, it wasn't. He wouldn't allow anyone to hurt her. Not ever. Where in hell did all this protectiveness come from? Usually, he liked to get under her skin, but lately…

Johnny turned to him, breaking into his thoughts, and thank goodness for that. He asked about his plans for the rest of the year. *Marriage* plans. It was easy enough to be noncommittal and hint at a future date next year. And tour plans, which were up in the air until he knew whether or not he'd win the starring role in *Sunday in Montana*. They were safe enough subjects and ones he didn't mind answering questions about. All the while, Gianna sat beside him, nodding and agreeing and being a pillar of support.

The interview lasted twenty minutes, an eternity on national morning shows. But it ended on a high note, with well wishes for the newly engaged couple and a plug for Gage's latest album.

On their way to the limo, Gage put his arm around her shoulder and whispered, "You did amazing. I couldn't have asked for a better interview. Mission accomplished."

Gianna had been the picture of grace and refinement. She gave the world a clear look at her life, and all that meant good press for him. She'd been a rock, impressing the hell out of him. So the arm around her shoulder wasn't just for show, but she'd never acknowledge that. She didn't want it there, if not for their little charade. It burned him a little to know she wouldn't give him the time of day otherwise.

"I was terrified," she admitted.

"You didn't seem like it. If your nerves were rattled, I couldn't tell. And that meant that viewers were eating it up."

"I'm just glad it's over with now."

They reached the limo, and the chauffeur opened the door. Gianna slipped in first, and then Gage followed, taking his seat and buckling up.

"Oh, boy. I can't wait to get these shoes off. They're too tight."

She pried them off immediately and sighed, massaging her ankles. How any woman could stand wearing those things always baffled him.

"Back to the hotel now, I've got research to do."

"Not just yet," Gage said. "I have a surprise for you."

"My feet hurt. I can't put those torture devices back on."

"No problem. We'll stop along the way and get you some comfortable shoes."

"I don't feel like shoe shopping."

"You're being difficult. It'll only take a minute. We'll get you some comfy tennis shoes. You're really going to like this surprise."

Gianna plopped back against the seat, her head cushioned by soft leather, and closed her eyes. "I don't like surprises," she mumbled, all her vim and vigor taking a break.

"You'll like this one. I guarantee it."

The interview behind her, Gianna's feet were happy now, encased in white tennies. She stood before the Nashville Parthenon in Centennial Park, the sign before her claiming the building to be the world's only exact-size replica of the original Greek Parthenon, dating back to 400 BC. This one was built in 1897 and was beyond a work of art. It was stunning, and something she'd had on her bucket list. Of course, she'd wanted to see the real thing, but this replica simply took her breath away.

Gage let her gape as long as she wanted, his eyes keen on her and not the structure before him, but she didn't care. It was a totally unexpected surprise. She didn't know why Gage went to the trouble. Well, maybe she did. He'd been asking a lot from her lately, and *taking* a lot from her. Like kisses that made her head spin and made her heart pound. The surprise had surprised her in its thoughtfulness. It was something he didn't have to do. And Gage Tremaine wasn't the kind of man who did things he didn't have to do. If he was reveling in that, so be it. He could tell her "I told you so" about her enjoying the surprise. But he didn't, and she appreciated that as well.

"It's the pride of Nashville, historically speaking," Gage said.

"And you knew I'd love to see it."

"We couldn't leave Nashville without you seeing it."

"It blows my mind." She got out her phone and began snapping pictures. "Brooke's gonna love this."

"You'll have to show her the inside, too."

Gage walked toward the entrance, and she followed. He didn't offer his hand. There were only a few visitors at the site, and he didn't press her about their charade. Chills ran up and down her spine as she took in her surroundings—marvels as far as the eye could see. Every time she saw something new and read the accompanying plaque, she became utterly enthralled. The tall columns surrounding her were indescribable. How on earth had the Greeks ever gotten them to their forty-five-foot height? And the sculptures along the walls were amazingly intricate and lifelike. She stared at the details for several minutes.

Gage came over to her. "Come with me," he said, this time taking her hand and tugging her away from the artwork.

They walked into the second room, and her eyes lifted to the towering gilded statue of Athena. It was massive and beautiful. "Heavens," she said.

"Athena, daughter of Zeus. I read somewhere she was Zeus's favorite child."

"She was strong. The protector of the city. Goddess of warfare," Gianna stated, remembering her Greek mythology.

"She was a lot like you, Gianna."

She turned her head from the statue to gaze at him. "Very funny."

"Not trying to be. She was the goddess of wisdom, too."

She blinked. Gage didn't usually come right out and compliment her. Not unless there was something in it for him. "You think I'm wise?"

"No, I think you're a goddess."

Laughter bubbled up and spilled over, echoing in the chamber. She should know better than to take him seriously.

Only Gage wasn't laughing with her. His sober eyes told a different story. One that brought goose bumps back to her arms. One that made her question why it was that she didn't like Gage all that much. He was all Texan, a hunk with deep-blue eyes, a man who looked at a woman and made her believe she was the only one on earth. It shattered her defenses. She didn't like that. Not at all. "Th-thank you for bringing me here, but we should go."

"I know, you have work to do."

"It's the truth. It's already been an exhausting day, and I'm a little behind schedule."

Gage nodded and put his hand to her lower back, ushering her outside. His constant touching for no good reason made her nerves jump. Not because she didn't enjoy it, but because she did. She walked over to another informational sign, pretending interest, and broke away from him. She didn't want her goose bumps to get goose bumps.

Relief registered immediately. He no longer touched her.

So why was she also terribly, terribly disappointed?

Gage tore up the page of lyrics he'd been writing and tossed it in the trash. Hell, he couldn't concentrate. His mind was on total shutdown. He'd made calls to industry friends and caught up on their news, but his heart wasn't really in it. He turned on the TV. Shut it off. Nothing interested him, not the classic Jimmy Stewart Western he'd seen a dozen times on the screen. Not even the script he'd brought along to look over from *Sunday in Montana*. He got up from the bed and paced back and forth in the hotel room, "wearing out the rug," as his mother would say. He was twitchy and restless. And the source of his restlessness came in the form of the woman in the bedroom ten feet away punching keys on her computer.

How could Gianna turn off the world so easily?

How could she shut him out and lose herself in her research when all he kept thinking about was how cute she looked in those doggone sneakers today? And how delighted she'd been to see the Parthenon. How good he'd felt bringing that joy to her, seeing her face light up, her eyes sparkle.

Brainiac, it's been five hours.

Of boredom.

Of being idle.

Of wanting to see her.

Needing a distraction, he ordered room service—a little bit of everything. Then he strode into the living room and poured himself a drink of the good stuff, bourbon that took time coursing down his throat, offering a slow, delicious burn all the way to his gut. It was good, damn good, but not enough to satisfy his edginess.

Not enough to quell his desire. He wanted Gianna. And not because she was here, convenient, and he was bored out of his mind. No, those were reasons to want other women. Women who wanted to hook up with a celeb. Women who didn't really know him. But not Gianna. She was different, special. He knew it as much as he knew the sun set in the west. And he knew it was wrong to want her.

Hell, he knew it and still he walked the steps to her bedroom door. He knocked, three sharp raps, and waited. "Gianna?"

"Just…a…sec," she said, distracted. She opened the door, and there she stood in a plush white robe, her hair slightly wet, glistening. She'd taken a shower and hadn't redressed. Those black-rimmed glasses perched on her nose told him she'd been working. Still.

"I'm starving." What was she wearing under that robe? And why did he find a cushy bathrobe and tangled, wet hair so damn attractive? He knew the answer, of course. Gianna, unassuming and so damn distracted, was the sexiest thing he'd ever seen. "It's after seven."

"Oh, I didn't realize."

"Lost in your work?"

"I only have another hour of—"

"I've ordered us room service. Should be here any minute."

"Thanks." She stared at him, blinking a few times. And he stared right back into those meadow-green eyes, watching her sweet mouth twist a little. How many times had he seen that particular look, as if she was trying to figure him out? Well, if she had a clue, she should tell him, because he didn't know why his feet weren't moving. Why he couldn't pull himself away from her doorway. He couldn't keep his heart from pounding hard, either. Or keep lust out of his eyes. And he didn't give a flying fig if she could read his mind.

She stood at the door, blocking the entrance as if she'd pulled guard duty. "Is there anything else?"

Her gaze lowered to his mouth, her eyes bold and daring. She was no longer distracted by her work. No, something else fascinated her; something else tempted her. They were inches apart, and raw tension pinged between them. He wouldn't make the first move. But he wouldn't back away, either. This was all Gianna. What she wanted. What they'd been tip-toeing around for days now. This chemistry between them. "Gage," she whispered.

"Right here."

"Maybe you shouldn't be." Yet there was no con-viction in her voice.

"Tell me to leave."

She pulled air into her lungs and opened her mouth. But the words didn't come. She reached up and put her hand to his cheek, stroked his face, gently, tenderly. A groan rose up this throat. She was play-ing with fire.

"I c-can't, Gage. I can't tell you to leave."

It was all he needed to hear. He cupped her face and positioned her mouth, their eyes meeting for a second of confirmation. They were doing this. And there was no protest, no refusal. He brought his mouth over hers and tasted her once, twice. A whimper rose from her throat, and then he took charge, pressing his lips to hers urgently, unleashing his pent-up lust on her. Consuming her with his mouth, his tongue.

Gage wanted more. He wanted everything from her, but he had to slow down. He couldn't rush her. He didn't want to overpower her. He wanted her to come along on this ride beside him. He wanted to please her, pleasure her. It wasn't just about reliev-ing his itch. It was more, because this was Gianna.

They kissed until they were breathless. Gage gave a kick to her door, opening it wider, and then he was backing her up, into the room, toward her bed. Her computer was on, papers all in a tidy pile on her desk. That was her, neat and tidy, and Gage wanted to see her let loose, watch her be free. Give her a reason to go wild.

He lowered her down onto the bed. Her hair spilled out around her, her eyes glowing. She untied the belt and he parted the robe, opening the material wide. His breathing stopped. "My God, Gianna. You're perfect."

Her skin was smooth and tan, creamy. Her small, beautifully rounded breasts filled the cups of her lacy white bra, and below she wore barely there matching panties.

He pulled off his shirt and tossed it, Gianna watching him carefully, her eyes wide and gleaming. She reached her arms out for him, and he nearly lost it. He was harder than granite under the zipper of his jeans, but determined to take this slow.

He lowered himself, and her arms came around his neck. He kissed her again and again, and those little noises she made down deep in her throat rocked him to his core. He touched the swell of her breasts, filling his hands, and he kissed her there over and over. Her nipples pebbled hard. Her breaths were coming sharp and quick, and he flattened his palm to her stomach and drew his hand down to touch her folds underneath her panties. A whimper rose from her throat, and he gave her more, sliding his fingers over her sensitized skin. Her hips arched up. Giving him access to do more, give her more. Panting, she squeezed out a plea. "Gage."

"I know, Gia, honey."

Her release came sharp and fast, her cries of pleasure echoing in his ears. He brought his mouth over hers again, and they shared one long, mind-blowing kiss.

A knock at the front door startled them. Ah, damn. Must be room service. "The food," he whispered. He hated that the moment was interrupted. "They'll leave it outside." No way was he getting up to eat now. Everything he wanted was laid out before him on this bed. "Are you okay?"

Gianna smiled, a satisfied lifting of her lips that told the whole story. "I'm very, very good."

He chuckled and pushed the hairs that had fallen onto her cheeks away from her face. "I'm very, very glad."

From the other room, his phone banged out a tune announcing a caller. He ignored it, hating this interruption even more. But the insistent thing wouldn't stop. "For heaven's sake," he said. "I'll get it."

"I'll watch you get it," Gianna said, rolling onto her side, all legs and creamy skin.

He chuckled again. He was impatient for her now, more than he thought possible.

He picked up the phone from the living room sofa. "You can leave it outside," he said, just barely holding on to his patience.

"Gage? Is that you?"

It was his brother. "Cade? What's up? Now's not a good time."

"No, it's not a good time. Mom's been in a car accident."

It was the last thing he expected to hear. "Crap. Is she okay?"

"She's unconscious."

Gage pinched his nose. He didn't want to hear this news. Blood rushed through his system. "What the hell happened? And where is she?"

"I'll explain all that later. Just come. We're at Juliet Memorial."

"Cade? How bad is it?"

"She's banged up, Gage. The doctor is in with her now."

"Okay, okay. I'll be there as soon as I can." He hung up the phone, his eyes slowly closing, and he envisioned his strong, beautiful mother lying in a hospital bed. Injured. Banged up. Frail.

"Gage?"

He turned, and Gianna walked into the room. She took one look at him, and immediately her smile faded. "What is it? What's wrong?" There was panic in her voice. She knew something serious was going on. She closed the lapels of her robe and came to stand beside him. "Gage, you're scaring me."

"Don't mean to."

"Then tell me. Now." More panic.

"It's my mom. She's been in a car accident. She's in the hospital."

"Oh, my God. No. Not Rose." Tears surged to her eyes, filling them with moisture. He had a feeling she was reliving another moment, a frightening one involving her own mother. She'd been so courageous, selflessly caring for her mom until the very end. It had been hard on her, and now this? It might be too much for her to take.

He wrapped her up in his arms, her soft robe pressing against his chest. He kissed her forehead. "Don't cry, Gia."

"I know. I'm sorry. I don't m-mean to make it w-worse. It's just a sh-shock."

"It is. I don't have details, but she's being treated. She hasn't woken up yet."

Gianna gasped. The noisy sound touched every part of him. She was suffering, too. She loved his mother. They both did.

"We have to go. I have to make arrangements."

"I'll get ready," she said softly. Yet she clung to him still, and every protective instinct he possessed didn't want to let her go. She needed comfort. And he wanted to give it to her. It pained him how much.

She broke away all on her own, giving him a brave nod, and strode into her room.

Gage used the speed dial on his phone and called Regan. She'd make the arrangements. She always knew what to do. If anyone could get him home quickly, it was her. And home was exactly where he needed to be.

Seven

"Would you like some coffee, Gianna?" Harper asked. "Cade and I are going to get some."

Gianna shifted in the uncomfortable hospital chair and shook her head. "No, thanks. I'm fine." But she wasn't fine. She'd been scared silly, and the fright had come far too close to home. She and Gage had flown in the dead of night to get to Juliet Memorial, Gage holding her hand the entire time, while she sent up prayers for Rose's recovery. Lily was in with the doctor now, discussing her mother's injuries. Time was creeping by.

Gianna glanced at Gage standing against the wall, speaking quietly to Regan. She'd gotten here before they had and greeted Gage with a big consoling hug. Gianna's heart had pinged then, a totally ridiculous emotion edging its way inside. She had no reason to be jealous. Regan was his manager. She was like a partner to him, too, and he didn't seem to make a move without her blessing. They were close. Gianna understood that, even though, whenever Regan was around, she totally monopolized Gage's time.

Now she had a hand on Gage's arm and they were face-to-face. He nodded his head as whatever she was saying seemed to resonate with him. She was his mentor, a person he relied on, but Gianna suspected Regan's interest in Gage went deeper than that.

But who was she to analyze his relationship with Regan when she couldn't figure out what the heck was happening between her and Gage? She didn't have a clue what had changed between them, except that spending time with him hadn't been horrible. In fact, he'd made their trip memorable. She'd had a good time at Red's, letting loose and dancing, eating decadent desserts and being Gage's sole focus while he sang about love.

The television interview had been difficult, but Gage made up for it with the surprise trip to the Parthenon. And afterward, in the hotel, she hadn't been able to resist him, hadn't been able to send him away. They'd combusted. She'd been unabashedly naked before him, stripped of her cement-hard resolve. And she was glad of it. He'd given her her very first orgasm.

Lily walked over to where the family was waiting. Cade and Harper set down their coffee cups, and Gage moved from the wall to greet her, Regan right by his side. Gianna stood as well, her pulse pounding, her legs wobbly.

"Mom's awake. She has a concussion, but the preliminary tests are showing no further injury. Her left arm is broken, and she has a bruised rib or two. The doctor will be out shortly to explain, but I know you guys were dying to find out. Looks like she's going to be okay."

Relieved sighs filled the room. Tears streaked down Gianna's cheeks. Lily and Harper were also wet puddles of thankful tears. Gage smiled for the first time since they'd learned of the accident. He walked over to her, leaving Regan to stand alone. "Good news, right?"

She nodded. "The very best."

"Are you okay, Gia?"

The pad of his thumb wiped away her tears. His touch also wiped away her worry. His touch made her feel safe. Which was odd, because nothing about Gage was safe. He was stubborn and confident and self-serving at times, and she'd never believed him a safe bet. Especially since they'd practically made love last night. But it wouldn't be fair to fault him for something she'd wanted. That she'd wanted him at all and desperately last night—now *that* was the bigger issue.

She stared into his eyes. "I should be asking you that question."

"I'm all right."

"Me, too. As long as Rose is going to recover, that's all that matters."

"She'll hate every minute of being laid up. You know my mom—she likes to be active."

"We'll entertain her."

Gage smiled, his eyes warm. "We will?"

"I'll do my best. I know she likes to play poker, and I'm pretty good myself."

"You are? I wouldn't have guessed," he said. "Gianna the card sharp."

"It's all about odds and numbers and logical choices."

"Leave it to you to suck the joy outta poker." He flashed a big smile, and she chuckled.

"What? No comeback? You must be exhausted."

"I'm pretty tired." Beat was more like it. It had been a mentally exhausting twenty-four hours.

"How about you go on home? Cade is taking Harper home, and they'll take you back."

"What about you?"

"I'm gonna stay a few more hours. I want to see Mom once they allow visitors. Lily will be here with me. And Regan. She's been working on rescheduling our LA trip."

Gianna had almost forgotten about that. They were supposed to make a few appearances in and around Hollywood this week. It was to beef up his good-guy image to the film studios.

She glanced across the room. Regan had her ear to a phone, speaking rapidly into the receiver, but her eyes were solely on Gage. Eyes didn't lie, Mama had always told her. *Words can deceive, but eyes are the entrance to the soul.*

A question was on her lips about his relationship with Regan, but now was not the time. And she wasn't really sure if she should be asking. Regan was an attractive single woman, if not several years older, and she certainly always had Gage's back, but it was none of Gianna's business. She was his temporary fake fiancée. Period.

It hadn't felt like that last night.

"I think that's a good idea. I'll come check on Rose later."

Gage kissed her cheek and nodded. "I'll tell Cade. Oh, and thanks for being here. Means a lot." He gave her hand a squeeze.

Regan slipped in between them, taking Gage's arm, gently grabbing his attention. "Now that we know your mama is going to be okay, I'd like to speak to you more about LA."

"Sure," he said. "Just let me talk to Cade and then I'm all yours."

Regan's expression brightened as if she'd just won a contest. She turned her way. "Gianna, you should get some rest. This must be hard on you."

"It's very hard," Gianna replied suggestively, focusing her full attention on Gage. "You have no idea."

Regan's triumphant expression faded. Her gaze shifted to Gage and then back to Gianna, weighing the innocent words and finally dismissing the innuendo.

Heavens, sometimes her quick wit needed reining in.

That was another thing Mama would warn her about.

But Gianna would rarely listen.

Noise from the living room woke Gianna from a restless sleep. Opening her eyes slowly, a glance at the clock on the nightstand confirmed she'd hadn't slept much, maybe a few hours. It was just before noon. She surveyed her surroundings. Every day she woke up in the Tremaine guesthouse, she had to remind herself about her current life situation. Pretending to be Gage's fiancée and living here was her new normal.

It was super weird going over the events of the past few days. From highs to lows. She was grateful that Rose's injuries weren't all that serious. Her prayers had been answered. Thank goodness. She got up and dressed in a pair of jeans and a cotton top, her actions quiet and precise. A glance in the mirror, and a few finger strokes to her hair, said it wasn't going to get much better than this without more effort. She didn't want to make the effort. Gage was back, and she wanted to hear an update on his mother.

She padded barefoot down the hall and into the living room. Gage sat on the sofa, his legs stretched out onto the coffee table, a cup of steaming brew in his hands. He lifted his lids to her, exhaustion written on his face.

"Hi," she said. "Did you just get home?" How strange was it to say those words to him? It was his home—it just wasn't hers. But Gage didn't immediately answer. He was too busy surveying her choice of clothes. His lazy blue gaze leisurely moved up and down her body. He approved, said the glimmer in his eyes. Jeans and a little cotton top earned her high marks—it just didn't make sense. Yet her insides warmed regardless.

"Just a few minutes ago. Did I wake you?"

"No," she fibbed. "I didn't sleep well."

He nodded. "I made coffee."

"Smells good. How's your mom?"

"Have some coffee and I'll tell you." He moved to rise.

She put up her hand. "No, please sit. I'll get it."

Gianna walked into the kitchen, poured herself a mug and came over to sit on the sofa beside him. She put her feet up, too, so there were two sets of toes on the rectangular cocktail table. They sipped coffee quietly and seemed to share an odd sense of peace, being there together. "So?"

"I got to see her. She's pretty banged up. Her face is bruised, and she's going to be sore for quite some time. They set her arm, and well, she's strong. She's not going to let this get the best of her. She was more worried about all of us and how we're doing."

"I get that. She's always been a mama bear. Did she explain how the accident happened?" All she knew was that Rose had lost control of her car and a telephone pole stopped her.

"She was driving home from town. It was dark on the road, and a dog suddenly appeared in her headlights. She swerved to keep from hitting it and ended up wrapped around a telephone pole."

"That's awful, Gage. And scary."

"No, it was actually a blessing. If that pole wasn't there to stop the car, she would've ended up in a ditch ten feet below. She was very lucky."

"Wow. I guess she was." Gianna sucked in a breath. Fate had a way of playing your hand for you. Luckily, this time Rose came out the winner. If one could say anything about getting in an accident was good luck.

"Gage, can I visit her?"

"Maybe later on tonight. She knows you were there, Gianna. She asked about you. But for now, the doctor wants her to rest. The pain meds knocked her out. She was sleeping when I left the hospital."

Tears threatened to spill. Knowing Rose had asked about her grabbed her heart and tugged hard. Rose was a special woman. With shaky hands, she set her mug down and willed herself to be strong. She couldn't fall apart in front of Gage again. He didn't need that.

"Hey," he said softly. He pulled her toward him, his powerful arms wrapping around her shoulders, her head naturally falling to his chest. She curled her feet onto the sofa, Gage her cushion. "Don't cry, Gianna."

"I'm usually not such a wuss."

He chuckled, his chest rising and falling, taking her with him for the ride. "Gia, you never could be. You're just weary. So am I. Close your eyes. Let's try to rest."

"Sounds good," she murmured, her eyes already closed. This time, she wasn't going to question how safe she felt in his arms. She was going to enjoy his comfort and hopefully fall into a blissful slumber, cocooned by his strength.

This wasn't a good idea, yet her needy body said otherwise.

She'd question all the reasons why she shouldn't be doing this, later.

And the list was long.

Afternoon light broke through the shutters in a dim glow, and Gianna woke gazing into a pair of drown-your-heart blue eyes. There wasn't a guy out there with more appealing ones. Beneath her was a rock-solid man, a man who cradled her in his arms—a man whose message below the waist could hardly be ignored.

Her pulse pounded. Her body buzzed.

He brushed hair away from her face and smiled. As if she hadn't just invaded his space, hadn't just slept on top of him for who knows how long. "How long have we been like this?"

"Awhile," he said, stroking her hair.

"You should've woken me," she whispered.

"You needed sleep."

"I'm so sorry." Her hands on his chest, she lifted up. But that only brought her waist down harder on his groin. His arousal couldn't be missed. He was turned on, but so was she. Heavens, she wouldn't lie about it. It would be too hard to pretend otherwise. Only the zippers of their jeans kept them from glory.

She should go before this got out of hand. But his look stopped her cold.

He cupped the back of her neck, the longing in his eyes unmistakable. He wanted to kiss her, and, in that moment, there was nothing she wanted more. She leaned in and he pressed his mouth to hers, his powerful kiss shutting off any hesitation she may have had. His touch was all-consuming. And oh, thank goodness for that.

"Remember what happened in the hotel room?" he whispered in her ear.

Her first genuine orgasm. How could she forget? She nodded, unable to form the words.

"We're going to finish that, Gia." He kissed her again, and little moans rose up from her throat. The pulsing of his body igniting hers. Red, fierce heat burned in her belly.

She shouldn't do this. Gage wasn't the man for her. He was too much like another man who'd let her down. Another man who'd hurt her. Charming, smug, overly confident. It was a secret she'd held close to her heart for so many years. A secret that burdened her heavily.

But Gage was too tempting, and back in that hotel room, he'd kindled a fire in her. He'd started something that needed finishing. Logic didn't play into this. No, this was about raw, sensual yearnings. This was about sex and satisfaction.

She ran a hand down his strong jaw, caressed the scruff and kissed him there. "Okay," she said softly.

A guttural noise sounded from his throat, a groan

touching every edge of her body, and he kissed her back, his tongue staking its claim. There was no turning back. She was going to give herself to Gage, and she was going to take what he offered her in return.

Gage ran his hands through her hair, lifting the tresses, letting them fall loosely about her shoulders. He unbuttoned her blouse, spreading it wide-open. Appreciation gleamed in his eyes, and she'd never felt like more of a woman.

He removed her blouse and bra, and beneath her, his arousal hardened. Quickly, he removed his shirt and tossed it away. He was all muscle and tiny chest hairs and broad shoulders.

"Touch me," he said, taking her wrists and bringing them to his chest. Her hands fanned out, her palms stroking over his torso. Moaning, he closed his eyes to the touch, and she continued to stroke him, to give him pleasure.

Gage cupped her breasts, kissing her there, palming her slowly, gently, until she was nearly out of her mind. He worked magic with his hands, his tongue, and then there was a frenzy to get naked. They needed to see each other fully, to touch and explore, to feel, soft to hard, and to taste everything.

Gage rolled her onto the side of the sofa and unzipped her jeans. He touched her aroused apex with his fingers and then slid the soft denim down her legs. She wiggled the rest of the way out of them, her body humming.

Gianna unzipped his jeans and then slid her hands inside to push them down, this turnaround being fair play. Her hand wound around his thick shaft and his hips arched. She stroked him, tasted him. "Damn," he gritted out.

And before she was entirely through with all the tasting and exploring, he stopped her, kissed her and then reached into his tossed-aside jeans for a condom. He was an expert at tearing it open quickly and fixing it over his manhood. She didn't want to know how he'd gotten so adept at it when Gianna had barely any experience at all.

Then she remembered that Gage wasn't just a family friend, he was a superstar and had beautiful women swarming him all the time. Probably. Most likely. *For sure.*

Gage kissed her again, and all those thoughts leaped out of her mind. He cupped her butt with one hand while playing over her thin, sensitive folds with the other. She was moist there already, but Gage fought for more. Clearly, he wasn't one to give up, and his stroking went on and on until she couldn't think, could barely breathe. She cried out, her body breaking apart, frenzied, wild. She tossed her head back, and Gage finished his fight. He made her shatter. He made her complete. He gave her another release, this one even more powerful than the first.

Gage waited for Gianna to come down to earth. It was amazing to see her break loose like that, but feeling it was even better. He was so damn ready for her, but his patience would pay off. Gianna wouldn't disappoint. She had no idea how beautiful she was, how her obvious lack of experience was such a turn-on to him.

She opened her eyes and smiled. "You okay, Brainiac?"

She nodded. "But we're not through yet."

He laughed. "Hardly."

He lifted her and set her over his hips so she straddled him. His hands on her waist, he helped lower her onto his shaft. She touched him once, twice, and he bucked, the sensation so damn good. The next time she moved on him, she took him deeper, and then deeper again. He was fully inside her on the next thrust, the red-hot pleasure bordering on pain.

He focused solely on her. There'd be no closing his eyes. Not this time. Gianna's olive-skinned body glistened, the sheen of sweat born of sex a heady thing. She moved easily on him now, meeting his thrusts and responding in kind. She tossed her head back, her hair flowing past her shoulders, the rosy tips of her breasts pointing skyward.

Gage couldn't hold back much longer. Sex with her was the best he'd ever had. She'd turned him on more than any woman he'd ever known. Ironically, he'd gotten a rep for being a bad boy, but he'd never tell that there'd only been six women in his entire life. Gianna being number seven. Lucky number seven.

She moved on him gracefully, meeting him thrust for thrust in a rhythm that was uniquely hers. He let her set the pace and loved how her instincts took over. She wasn't shy. She gave him what he craved, moving her hips, gyrating to produce the maximum pleasure. His body was on edge. He needed more, and he guided her hips down on him faster, harder. Her eyes closed, she found a faster pace. She gave herself to him without question and moved with his every thrust, his every buck. Then her eyes opened again, wide with surprise and filled with lust. Her mouth dropped open and she whispered, "Gage."

"Let go," he said, completely awed.

Her eyes squeezed shut then, and she trembled fiercely, the force of her release beautiful to watch.

Gage brought her down, into his arms, and laid her on the sofa. Coming up and over her, he rained kisses onto her sweet face and finally finished what they'd started in Nashville, taking them both home.

Eight

Gage held Gianna's hand as they entered Juliet Memorial together. They walked down the hall and entered the elevator. He kept her close by his side. Was it for the sake of appearances or because he wanted to keep them connected? Even wondering why, she couldn't break away, couldn't puzzle out what she was feeling inside. How could she look at Rose with a straight face without revealing what had happened between them? How does one behave after having earth-shattering sex with a man? She didn't know, because after getting dressed, they'd rushed out of the guesthouse, Gage on the phone with Regan for most of the time.

They reached Rose's hospital room door. "Do you

want to go in first?" he asked. "Or do you want to go in together?"

"First," she said, guilt making her cringe inside. She didn't want to deny Gage this time with his mother, but it would be easier to face Rose alone. Plus, now that she was feeling things for Gage, things she didn't want to name, there was something she needed clarification from Rose about—something from her past. Now that her mom was gone, Rose was her only hope in putting some skeletons to rest.

Gage didn't react other than giving her a nod. "Have a good visit," he said and placed a quick kiss to her forehead.

There was a buzz surrounding them, a heat, a current that made her dizzy, made her question everything in her life. What was she doing with this man? "Gage?"

"It's gonna be okay," he said. "Trust me."

But did she? Did she trust Gage Tremaine? Too many questions popped into her mind, too many memories of Gage not being trustworthy. Of him teasing her and picking on her and trying to make her feel inferior. But that was a lifetime ago. That was when they were kids, teens. That wasn't now.

She turned and entered the room. Sterile surroundings, the smell of alcohol and disinfectant, greeted her. Flowers brightened the room, arrangements of sunflowers and daisies and roses—lots of roses.

The woman she'd come here to see gave her a sweet smile. "Gianna."

She strode over to the bed and carefully sat down on the very edge. "How are you, Rose?"

Gianna had never seen Rose looking so frail and wounded. Like a little bird. Tucked into covers, hiding most of her injuries, she sat up straighter and winced. Gianna felt her pain down to her toes. "As you can see, sweet girl, I'm mending. But slowly."

"I'm so sorry you were hurt. You really gave us all a scare."

"And I'm sorry, too, for you. Losing Tonette and now me being in the hospital."

"I'm not the one with a broken arm and bruised ribs. No need to be sorry. It couldn't be helped. If anything, you saved a dog's life."

"Yes, and I'd probably do it again."

"Well," Gianna said. "I brought you chocolates." She cleared her throat. "Actually, they're from Gage, too. We stopped in town and got you your favorites." She pulled a lavender box with gold lettering out of her purse and set it on the table tray.

"Thank you. That's sweet."

She put out her hand, and Gianna covered it with her own. "How are you and my son holding up?"

Gianna's face flamed. She put her head down. Her relationship with the truth was being tested again and again. "We're fine. Things went well in Nashville. The interview went better than I could've hoped, and that's good because it's the only one I'm *ever* doing." She smiled, grateful to be here speaking to Rose. "You have no idea how worried we were when we got the news about your accident."

"I'm going to be fine, don't you worry." Rose squeezed her hand. "I'm tougher than I look."

Tears welled in her eyes and she was hopeless trying to hide them. "I know. Thank God for that." She couldn't bear to even think about losing Rose, too.

"Gianna? Is there something else troubling you? Is it Gage?"

"No. It's not about Gage." She'd been haunted by a question, a secret and now that her mother was gone, only Rose would know the answer. "It's about my…father."

Rose blinked and stared out the window. "Your father?"

"Yes, my father." *He* was the man who had betrayed her and her mother. The man who kept her from going all in with Gage. "You see, I found these letters, years ago. They were correspondence between my mother and father. Secret letters. Do you know about this, Rose?"

Rose sighed and turned back to face her. "Yes, I know about your mother and father. I'm the only one who knows the truth. And I swore to your mother I wouldn't tell you."

"It's okay, Rose. I already know. I was fifteen when I found and read the letters. My mother never knew. I never told her."

"Why? Why didn't you confront her when you had the chance?"

"Because I knew how much my mother wanted me to believe the fantasy. That they had a loving relationship and we had a perfect family. My mother didn't want to disillusion me. She didn't want me to blame myself for my father leaving us. Abandoning his family."

Rose nodded. "It was important to her that you'd never feel the same pain she'd felt when he ran off with another woman. It was easier to let you believe he had died tragically. As strange as it sounds. Tonette loved you so much, she couldn't hurt you that way."

"I know. That's why I never asked her about it. I never confronted her about the lies she told me. I mean, those letters explained the whole story. He didn't want any part of her, or me."

"She wanted to tell you once you'd grown up, but she was proud of what you'd accomplished in your life and didn't want to upset anything. I don't know, maybe she was scared or worried about telling you."

"Is he still alive?"

"No, he died several years ago. He'd moved to Europe and married a wealthy woman. He'd written to your mom for only one year, and then the letters stopped coming. She was glad of it. Those letters only upset her. Once your mom washed her hands of him, she was a new woman. A stronger woman, like you." Rose gave her hand another gentle squeeze. "I'm sorry about all this."

"I'm fine with it. I made my peace with it years ago. But I do want to know one thing—what was my father like? Can you tell me about him?"

"Uh, yes. I can tell you he was handsome as the devil. Joe Marino was extremely charming and funny when it suited him. He was a man any woman would find hard to resist. But he was also selfish, Gianna. He always wanted what he couldn't have. And once he got it, he discarded it like yesterday's trash. Tonette fell victim to him immediately. Oh, she loved him so, and he broke her heart. I'd say they had three good years of marriage, but then your father got restless. He was an attention seeker and wanted the focus back on himself."

"Wow. I guess I figured all that from the letters, but hearing it now from you makes it all real."

"Your mama always said you were the best thing to come out of the marriage."

Gianna's heart lurched. "I'd have to agree. Thank you, Rose."

"You're welcome, sweetie. And for what it's worth, I think you did the right thing by going along with your mom. She wanted to protect you. It was important to her."

A few taps at the door brought her head around, and Gage appeared at the threshold. "Is all the girl talk done?"

"Come in, Gage," Rose said. "We've had a nice chat."

Rose met her eyes and she nodded. "Yes, we have."

"Anytime you want to talk again, just let me know," Rose told her softly. She appreciated the talk and the truth.

She rose from the bed just as Gage made his way into the room. Gage kissed his mother on the cheek. "Hi, Mom. How's the patient doing?"

"She's busted up some, but anxious to get out of this bed."

Gage took a position right beside Gianna, his arm curling around her back. She moved slightly out of his reach and stood her ground. She couldn't have him touching her. Not in front of Rose. She was too astute, too perceptive.

"One more day and you can come home, Mom."

"I'd better come home. I'm going to dance at Cade's wedding. Arm in a cast or not."

Gianna chuckled. Rose had spunk, and thank goodness she wasn't as badly injured as they'd originally thought. Her bruises would heal—her rib would heal, too. She'd have to deal with a broken arm, but if anyone could manage, it would be Rose.

"And I'll be the first one to whisk you around on the dance floor," Gage said.

Rose smiled and darted curious glances between the two of them. Gianna was afraid she'd ask a question they couldn't answer. That she'd find out they'd given in to desire. It would worry Rose, and that was the last thing she needed right now. "I'll let you two talk. I'll wait for you outside, Gage," she said. She kissed Rose's cheek. "Try to get some rest."

"I will, and you take care, too. Thanks for visiting, sweetheart."

"Of course. I'll see you tomorrow."

"I'll only be a few minutes," Gage announced. She gave him a slight nod and turned away.

She found the restroom and splashed cold water on her face. It didn't help. It didn't clear her mind. She was confused about a lot of things. And she hated being out of control like that. She hated not looking at Gage rationally and seeing the situation for what it was. She was usually more logical, more sensible about things. But after making love with Gage, she'd learned something about herself she hadn't known. She was vulnerable to him, his charm. He'd done things to her body that no man ever had. He'd made her feel womanly and alluring, all things she hadn't thought important. Or necessary. Yet those were wonderful feelings.

But was Gage a man like her father? Gage hadn't had long-lasting relationships with women. From what Lily had told her, he'd never been in love. Was he too self-centered to put someone above himself?

Ten minutes later, Gage entered the waiting room, and their eyes met. "Hi. Mom's resting now."

"That's good," she said, her shoulders stiffening up. Images of Gage naked and gorgeous, touching her, making her cry out, entered her head. When he was in the room, she could hardly think of anything else. "She needs her rest."

"Hopefully, she'll come home tomorrow."

She nodded and stood. "Are you ready to head back? I have work to finish."

Gage laughed under his breath. He rubbed at his chin and then eyed her. "You're dedicated, I'll say that."

"You know I am."

"I also know a lot of things about you I didn't know before."

Gianna wouldn't take the bait. She put her purse strap over her shoulder and walked past him. "Are you coming?" she asked, walking out of the room.

Gage caught up to her in three strides and grabbed her hand. "I go where you go," he teased.

"You've got that backward, don't you?"

"After this afternoon, Gianna, I'm not so sure."

More images flashed of being naked with him. She pulled away from his grip, but he held tight. "The hospital is kinda crowded now. Lots of eyes on us," he whispered in her ear, "and we're a couple, remember?" He tightened his grip on her hand, and goose bumps popped up on her arms. They were back to faking it.

She ground her teeth.

He was impossible.

He was sexy.

He was charming.

It was a combustible combination.

Gage exited the Aston Martin and came around to open the door for her, his Southern manners never taking a back seat to his charm. She'd have preferred to open her own car door, but it wasn't worth the argument. Gage wouldn't agree. They hadn't said much on the way home from the hospital, Gage turning up the radio and singing along with the music. He was carefree and loose, as if his world was going according to plan. She often wished she could let go like that just once. But it wasn't in her DNA. She planned things out, needed to know where she was going at all times. And Gage had disrupted that order in her life.

She entered the house and tossed her purse on the sofa, Gage only steps behind her. She was about to turn his way, but two strong arms wrapped around her waist and pulled her close from behind. The subtle sent of his cologne wafted by, and his warm breath fanned over her throat. "I know you have work to do, but when you're done, I'll be in my room."

She turned in his arms to face him, his eyes deep, dark blue and dangerous. "Gage, we can't—"

He brushed his lips over hers, once, twice, and the familiar taste of him was too hard to resist. The promise of what he offered too hard to refuse. She circled her arms around his neck and kissed him back. His hands roamed over her body, gentle caresses that sent shivers up and down her spine.

Gage stopped kissing her and pulled himself away. "Gianna, just go, do your work," he rasped. "I meant what I said. I'll be waiting. It's your choice."

And then Gage walked out of the room, leaving her trembling, her lips swollen, her body on the brink.

Her legs wobbly, she walked into her room and sat down at her computer. She had a dozen pages of notes to compile into some semblance of order for her workshop. For the first time in a long time, she wasn't thrilled with doing her work. She went through the notes in a kind of trance, trying to focus on their importance, trying to make order out of it all. Usually, she had no trouble deciphering her scribbles. Usually, she found solace in her research, enjoyed putting cohesive and orderly bullet points to paper. "What is wrong with me?" she muttered.

It wasn't rocket science.

Gage had awakened her. He'd shown her how making love should be between a man and woman. Her head was filled with images of him, of them together. Would she ever look at him in the same way?

He wasn't right for her. They were as different as night and day. But she'd learned something from him. Big shock. He'd actually taught her something. That making love and being in love were two different things. He'd taught her that lust wasn't love. It was desire, wanton desire. And it dealt more with the pleasures of the flesh than any real emotion.

Intellectually, she'd known that. Good God, she'd given lectures about human nature and relationships, but what she hadn't known until this moment was that it could pertain to her. That knowing Gage was in his room, waiting for her and willing to give her another night of, well…orgasms, made her lose her focus on work, her concentration shot.

She shut down the computer. No work was to be had today. She debated for half a second about her next move. Then she slid on her boots, tossed on a lightweight jacket and exited her room.

She stopped up short, spotting Gage on his way to the kitchen. He wore faded jeans and an unbuttoned shirt. If there was a female heaven, he was it.

He took one look at her and asked, "Going somewhere?"

"Out."

"Out where?"

"Just out." She'd planned on saddling a horse and

riding out. It was a foolish idea. The sun had already set, and she wasn't that experienced a rider. Besides, what did she know about saddling a horse? Nathan was probably off duty by now. It wasn't like her to just…react and not make a solid plan. It was Gage's fault. He made her dizzy. And one thing Gianna was not normally was dizzy.

"Running, Gianna?"

"In boots?" she quipped.

His lips cocked up. "Not the kind of running I meant."

Her shoulders slumped, and a deep sigh pushed out of her mouth. "Gage, I'm not this convenient little toy you can play with."

"You're right. Nothing about you is convenient, Gia," he said softly. He wasn't mocking her. Not this time. "Did you finish your work?"

"No. I can't concentrate." Why did she admit that to him? Sometimes her relationship with the truth got her in trouble.

He sighed and ran a hand through his hair. The strands fell back into place, except for a thick chunk that landed just over his right brow. She had an urge to push it back in place and run her fingers through the rest of his dark locks. Not a safe train of thought.

"I was just getting some ice cream. Want some?" he asked.

"No. Yes. Uh…" She stared at the opening of his shirt, the thin strip of muscle and bronzed skin peeking out. Taunting her. Tempting her.

"It's not a hard question, Gianna. Either you want some or you don't."

She lifted her lids to him. "I want some."

Gage didn't react. He simply took her hand and led her into the kitchen. She took a seat while he opened cabinets, took out two cartons of ice cream from the freezer and scooped up a big dish of chocolate and strawberry, topping the mound with nuts and caramel sauce. He set out one dish, two spoons. "Have at it."

His eyes were on her, so clear, so blue. He picked up his spoon and dug in. As he swallowed, a delicious groan rose up his throat, and suddenly she didn't want ice cream anymore. She wanted to make him groan. She wanted to be that girl who could throw aside her misgivings for once. She wanted to give in to what she was feeling, her rigid rules and vows be damned.

She'd been fighting it, her logical brain battling her vulnerable heart.

She picked up the dish, grabbed his spoon, along with hers, and whispered, "Follow me."

Gage was smart enough not to be shocked—or not to let on if he was. Sometimes he knew her better than she knew herself.

She walked into his room and turned to him. He grabbed the dish out of her hands and set it aside. His arms came around her, drawing her up so close they breathed the same air. Her heart beat crazy fast, and she smiled from the depths of her soul. He smothered her smile with kisses, demanding and potent. Welcome kisses she'd craved. "Gia, sweetheart, I didn't think I could spend another night in this bed without you."

"Same," she said. With that one word, she surrendered herself to him. She was through fighting him.

And she was free at last. Liberated from what she perceived as the right thing. She only had to answer to herself, and she was all in.

Completely in. With Gage Tremaine.

Who would've ever thunk it?

Gage lay lazily beside Gianna now, his naked body close to hers. They'd napped after another burned-into-his-memory bout of sex earlier. They'd totally forgotten about the ice cream, which was now a creamy puddle in the bowl.

Gianna had no idea how she demolished him. Her body, her mind, those funky glasses, all turned him on. But he was greedy. He wanted more. He wanted to take it slow with her. To show her another side of him, the easy side of sex.

He ran his hand along Gianna's leg, starting at the ankle and slowly moving up, past her knee, to the creaminess of her slender thigh. His fingers spreading wide, he needed to touch every inch of her body. Caressing her was instinctive; his hands and mouth knew what she liked and how she liked it.

His fingertips feathered over her apex, and she stirred. She was so damn responsive to him.

"Gage," she murmured, her eyes closed.

"Shh, sweetheart. Just let me touch you."

He fanned over her flat belly and touched the tip

of his finger to her navel, circling it once, twice. His palm flat, he moved up her torso and teased the underside of her breasts. Then he flattened one breast gently, enjoying the soft, rounded mound in his hand. Cupping her, he gave her breast one gentle squeeze. He took his time pleasuring her there, pebbling the very tips and tasting them with his tongue.

Gianna stirred again, arching her hips, a little whimper rising from her throat.

Oh, man. Her sexy sounds moved him more than he thought possible. He was solid rock below the waist but determined to see this through.

He slid his hand behind her head and gave her a long, slow, delicious kiss. Then another one, and one more. Slowly, deliberately, lovingly.

He whispered sweet words in her ear, telling her she was beautiful and sexy and how he was going to make love to her slowly.

She moaned her responses.

All the while, Gage held back and waited until the moment was right. Then he covered her body, teasing his manhood over her, and she bucked. It was torture for him, too.

He gave her a little more of himself. And then more again. She moved with him, slowly, patiently. It was heaven and hell at the same time. Holding back, he moved in deep and continued to go slow, to let her absorb the sensations. To feel how good it was between them.

She clutched his shoulders and they moved together, unhurried and deliberate, her pace matching his. But then the moment came and Gianna gritted her teeth, her body sharpening, her release ready. It killed him to keep the pace slow and easy when all he wanted to do was take the ride with her. She shuddered as he continued to stroke her slowly, her climax coming in one long, drawn-out, amazing wave. It was worth the effort. She was sated. Pleasured and awed. It was all expressed on her beautiful face, in her pale green eyes.

Gage took his relief, too, and then wrapped her up in his arms.

"Thank you," she said softly.

"I should be thanking you, Brainiac." He kissed her and again couldn't believe that Gianna Marino was a hidden treasure he had been lucky enough to find.

He just didn't know if he could keep her.

Or if he should.

"I didn't mean to keep you from going to LA with Gage."

Rose had insisted on having afternoon tea outside under the shade of a giant oak tree in the backyard. They sat on comfortable lawn chairs overlooking the Tremaine property. It was good for Rose to be outdoors. She'd been recuperating inside for days and needed the fresh air, so Gianna went along with it. "I know you were planning on doing some traveling with him. And LA is an exciting place," Rose said.

"I suppose it is, but I'll see it another time."

LA might be exciting, but not more than the past

week she'd had with Gage. If they weren't out in public or keeping Rose company up in her room, they
were holed up in the guesthouse, making love morning and night. They'd been insatiable with each other.
Sex with Gage was incredible. And she loved waking
up in his arms every morning, but they'd both agreed
it would be better for Gianna to stay home this trip. To
be with Rose for the next few days. Lily and Harper
were knee-deep in wedding plans, the wedding only
a month away now, and Cade was working long hours
to clear up his schedule for his honeymoon.

"I'm happy to be here with you. I don't think Gage
really needed me on this trip. Regan is with him, and
it's all supposed to be behind-the-scenes stuff. Meet-
ings with producers and such. I think he's doing one
television interview. Thank goodness they don't need
me for that."

"Hmm." Rose sipped her tea. "So you and Gage
are getting along better now?"

Gianna paused, her heartbeat speeding up. "Uh,
yes. We weren't really *not* getting along."

Rose studied her, searching her eyes. "Gianna, I
don't mean to pry. You're both adults."

"Rose, it's okay. I can assure you we're sticking to
the plan. Everything's okay."

"Good. That's all I need to know."

It wasn't like she was going to fall madly in
love with Gage or anything. That would be foolish
and illogical. No, they were simply having a fling,
something Gianna had never done before. She was

determined to keep it simple and easy. Just a few more weeks of this, and they'd go on their separate paths.

Gianna sipped tea and smiled at Rose, yet a pesky little notion flashed into her mind.

Was she lying to Rose? Or, worse yet, was she lying to herself?

She missed Gage like crazy. It wasn't just about their fling. He was becoming important to her. He'd been gone for twenty-four hours already, and she hadn't heard a word from him. It was strange. She hadn't expected him to ignore her.

She was, after all, his fake fiancée.

"How is your work going, Gianna?"

"I'm happy to say I'm almost finished with my workshop. I'll be giving the seminar Friday night at the university. I was honored to be asked to participate in this special summer series Fairmont is offering."

"I know you've been working hard on it."

"It's a passion of mine, so it wasn't that difficult. I enjoy doing it."

Gage had promised to come, which was sweet of him, but was it out of support for her or to make yet one more public appearance as a couple?

After tea, Gianna spent the rest of the afternoon putting the finishing touches on her seminar. Her three-hour workshop devoted an entire hour to trust in relationships. She had examples and data that proved that trust was one of the key factors in sustaining a good family dynamic.

This one hit close to home due to her family history. Her mother had placed her faith and trust in her father, and he had abandoned them. And her mom had chosen to cover it up. She couldn't fault her mother. But the tiniest part of her wished her mom would've trusted her with the truth.

Her phone buzzed, and she checked the message. The text was from Gage. Her heart raced as she opened the message.

Busy here, going nonstop. Staying an extra day. Be home Saturday. Sorry to miss your seminar. Will make it up to you, Gage.

Her shoulders slumped, and her eyes stung. It wasn't what Gage had said or the rushed way he'd said it that put a knot in her gut. It was what he didn't say. And he wasn't coming to her presentation on Friday evening.

She should be fine with this. Having Gage gone meant less pretending, less deception, and yet dire disappointment washed over her. What had she expected? Roses and chocolates? Claims of love and adoration? No. But at least he could've asked about her well-being. He could've been more considerate. Heck, after all they'd shared, he should've picked up the phone and called her.

The phone in her hand, her fingers itching to respond, her mind filled with snarky comebacks. "Gee, thanks for the split second of your time." Or, "Don't worry about my seminar, I've only worked on it all summer." And her best one: "Brickhead, what on earth is wrong with you?"

She didn't send any one of those texts. Instead, her pride took hold and she simply wrote, See you on Saturday, Gianna.

Her mother used to say, "The heart wants what the heart wants."

Gianna never believed it, though. She was far more rational than that. She never truly believed the heart could take over the mind.

Until now.

She missed her mother.

She missed Gage.

She hit Send on her phone and then flopped onto the sofa.

And burst into tears.

Nine

Gage sat on his LA hotel room bed, staring at his phone. It was late, past ten in Texas. Gianna had probably gone to bed already. He wanted to believe that. Crap. No, he didn't. He itched to punch in the numbers that would bring Gianna's sweet voice to his ears. He itched to speak to her, to tell her how his day went. To ask her how hers went. Hell, he'd texted her when he'd first arrived here a couple of days ago. The message looked like a mindless scribble. But it wasn't. He'd taken a good long time coming up with that message. A message within a message. Damn, his hand trembled trying to come up with the right thing to do. The woman had him reduced to shaking in his boots. He couldn't give her the common courtesy of a "Hi, been thinking of you. Been missing you."

No. Not him. He was running scared. Feeling things for Gianna he shouldn't feel. When he was with her, his willpower evaporated. He couldn't see straight. He couldn't think straight. He craved her body, her sharp wit, her sassy mouth. But now that they were apart, he saw things more clearly. They were apples and oranges. They were oil and water. They were fly-by-the-seat-of-his-pants musician and common sense–intellectual professor.

Sexy professor.

They were *not* two peas in a pod.

He'd made a vow to his mother to tread carefully around the grieving Gianna. To make sure he didn't hurt her. And what had he done? The first chance he got, he'd broken that vow. Shoot, he'd really blown it.

Someone knocked on his door. Whatever they were selling, he didn't want, but the light tapping continued. He rose from his bed and slipped his arms into a shirt. "I'm coming."

He peered through the peephole and then yanked open the door. "Regan?"

"Hi, hope it's not too late for you?" His gaze slid to the champagne bottle and two glass flutes she held in her hand. She wore some sort of stretchy knit dress, her blond locks down around her shoulders.

"Late for what?"

"To celebrate, silly." She slunk past him and entered the room. "Don't worry, no one saw me come in."

Having a woman in his hotel room after hours wouldn't look cool, even if she was his manager and business partner. Regan usually didn't make late-night calls like this.

"What are we celebrating?" he asked.

"Everything." She sat down on his bed and crossed her legs. "Your screen test went really well today. I overheard the producers talking, Gage. You and Leah Marie had great onscreen chemistry. I think you won the part."

"Think?"

"Well, we can't be certain until they make us an offer. But our little scheme may just have worked. You and Gianna are pretty convincing. The producers like that you're getting married to a professional woman. It's good publicity for the movie."

He supposed it was good news. It's what he'd been hoping to hear. So why did it feel like a rock just dropped in the pit of his stomach?

"Let's drink a toast, Gage. Would you open the bottle for me?"

Regan had worked so hard for him all these years. He wouldn't have a career if it wasn't for her. He couldn't refuse one drink, even though champagne was not, and would never be, his drink of choice. "Sure. I guess one drink won't hurt."

He sat down beside her and took the bottle from her hand. She grabbed his arm. "Gage, I wish you'd smile. You look like you're going to your own execution."

He smiled for her sake. "Sorry. I'm a bit tired. We've had a busy day, is all."

"We have, but I loved every minute of it. Remember, it's black-tie tomorrow night at the charity event."

"I don't really want to go. Any way we can skip it? It's the night of Gianna's seminar, and I promised her I'd be there. I kinda feel like a heel after all she's doing for me."

"The bookworm will understand, Gage. That's really not your thing, now is it?"

The bookworm? His gut tightened. He didn't like hearing her described that way. Even if he'd teased her most of his life, it was a private thing between the two of them. Brickhead and Brainiac, what a team they made. "She's a lot more than that." Hell, his voice had gone to an irritated pitch.

Regan stared at him, her brows gathering, her face going beet red. "Don't tell me you're falling for her? Gage, she doesn't fit into our world."

He put his head down. She wasn't saying anything he didn't already know. He hated hearing it, though. "Regan, lay off, okay? She's just a good friend."

"You need to remember that more than I do." Regan gave his hand a squeeze. "And yes, we have to show up at the party tomorrow night. It's Leah Marie's famous charity event. You know how she is about rescuing cats. She's the star of the movie. We have to make nice."

Make nice? He wanted to make nice with Gianna. The whole time Regan was in his hotel room, on his bed, he was thinking of his fake fiancée and all the things they could be doing to each other right now.

But even more so, he just wanted to hear the soft lull of her voice.

He ushered Regan out of his room twenty minutes later, grateful to have her gone. He had some serious thinking to do about Gianna. He'd been cold to her. That text he'd sent was meant to put her off, but all it had succeeded in doing was wash him with guilt. A good, hard scrubbing of it. He'd thought he was doing the right thing, but now he wasn't sure.

He missed her.

Wanted to talk to her.

Needed to hear her voice.

Man, he had it bad.

Gage's voice crooned in her ear, his specific ringtone waking her up from a sound sleep. She glanced at the clock on her nightstand. It was after eleven. Popping straight up, she nibbled on her lips. Why was Gage calling so late? Had something happened? Through the darkness, she scrounged around for her phone and finally came up with it. She pushed the button. "Hello, Gage?"

"Hi, Gia." His voice was mellow and sweet and…

"Why are you calling so late? Is everything okay?"

"Everything's fine, sweetheart. Sorry if I woke you."

Sweetheart? "It's okay, I guess. I mean, I was sleeping, but now I'm up and so—"

"How are you?"

"Me? I'm doing fine."

"That's good. I have to apologize for not calling sooner. I, uh, I have no excuse, really."

She sat up straighter on the bed. It was intimate speaking to him in total darkness. "So why are you calling now?"

"The truth?" he said ever so softly.

"If you can manage it." She wasn't letting him off so easily.

"I missed you. I needed to hear your voice, Gia."

She squeezed her eyes shut. Did he know what he was doing to her? Did he know that hearing him admit that sent her heart soaring? "Why, Gage? Why call now?"

"Because I've been acting like a jerk," he said, keeping his tone soft, even. "I've been trying to keep a promise I made."

"What promise?"

"Not to hurt you."

"Oh, so you promised your mother you wouldn't hurt me, and you thought pushing me away was the answer?"

"I never meant to push you away. It's just when I got here, I told myself it was for the best that we steer clear of each other unless we were pretending to be engaged. I'd convinced myself of it, and it was only easy for about half a minute. The rest has been a struggle."

"What are you saying?"

"I'm saying I never expected this to happen, this crazy pull I have to you."

"I never expected anything like this, either."

"I miss you like crazy, Gianna. I wish you were here with me right now."

She wasn't exactly sure where this was leading. Did he miss his bed buddy? Or was he speaking straight from the heart? "I miss you, too," she whispered.

"Good," he said, relief in his voice.

"Good?" She chuckled at his logic. "Why good?"

"Gianna, there are things I want to tell you. Things I want to say, but not over the phone. When I see you in person, we'll talk."

The hope and promise in his voice stunned her. His sincere tone meant so very much to her. He'd tried pushing her away and couldn't do it. He missed her. He'd been a jerk to her—he'd admitted it—and she'd forgiven him for that. Tears welled in her eyes.

And then it hit her.

Why her emotions were in shreds, running high and low.

Why she'd been so darn angry with him.

She loved him. She'd fallen in love with her childhood nemesis, the boy who'd teased her mercilessly, the man who'd made her body sing, over and over again.

She loved Gage Tremaine. It slid over her like a beautiful waterfall, cascading over every inch of her body, wetting her mind with endless possibilities. Her and Gage. Gage and her. Her mother had been right.

The heart wants what the heart wants.

"Are you tired?" he asked.

Not anymore. "No."

"And you're in bed?"

"I am."

"What are you wearing, sweetheart?" he drawled, all tall, sexy Texan.

"Wouldn't you like to know?"

"I'm picturing your university shirt, you know the one. Actually, that's not true. I'm picturing it off you, my hands on your soft skin."

"Gage?" Her body reacted, his words turning her on.

"I'm sorry, Gia. But my imagination is kinda going wild."

"I like wild," she whispered.

"I know you do. Wanna do something wild right now?"

With him? "Yes. What do you have in mind?"

"This one time, Brainiac, keep your mind out of this and...*just feel*. Are you with me, Gia?"

Shivers ran down her spine, the anticipation killing her. "I'm with you, Gage." She was with him all the way.

And inside, her heart was brimming with love, making her more vulnerable than ever before.

Gianna stood at the podium in the Fairmont lecture hall and looked out at the students beginning to fill the seats. It was a bigger crowd than she'd expected. She wouldn't fool herself into believing that her Family Studies seminar was the sole attraction to the hall. No, many of the students were here out of curiosity. They wanted to see the woman who'd stolen country superstar and onetime bad boy Gage Tremaine's heart. They wanted to see the woman who had tamed the beast. She laughed silently at that. Just who was taming whom last night during their *phone call* has yet to be determined. But the students were here and hopefully they would learn a thing or two.

Thinking of Gage made her heart ping. He'd called earlier in the afternoon to wish her good luck. To say that he'd wanted to be there for her, but Regan felt the charity event with big-name celebrities was too important a deal to blow off. Gianna had given him a pass on it. Just knowing he cared was enough for her.

Lily and Harper sat in the first row. They gave her a little wave, and she smiled at them. Rose had wanted to come, but sitting in a hard-back university chair for three hours would be difficult for her. Luckily, the three of them banded together and Rose had backed down.

Once the doors were closed and the room was filled to near capacity, Gianna dug deep into her lungs for breath. Her months of hard work and research were about to pay off now. Behind her was a screen that would show her PowerPoint presentation. She spoke into the podium mic.

"Welcome, everyone. I want to thank you all for being here. I know it's summer, and you have many other things going on in your lives, so the fact that you're here today means you're serious about the subject. Today, we'll cover relationships with loved ones, family dynamics and how the ever-changing world challenges and influences the family unit. We'll discuss the importance of understanding, trust and truth using real-life scenarios and examine how lives are often greatly impacted by the three.

"Let me begin by speaking about the power of understanding…"

Gianna continued on, highlighting the most important aspects of her workshop using the PowerPoint graphs behind her. The stats cemented her research and laid the foundation for each of her topics.

Midway through her course, she gave her students a ten-minute break. As she tidied up her notes, her colleague Timothy Bellamy walked over to her to congratulate her on the workshop so far, and on her engagement. She'd noticed him in the audience wearing a three-piece suite, listening intently. His praise meant something to her. She respected his opinion, but suddenly it dawned on her, that what she'd felt for him in the past was miniscule compared to the way she felt about Gage. Brilliant college professor versus sex god country rock star? Maybe that's how others would look at it, but now Gage was so much more to her than that. And wasn't that the biggest surprise of all?

After her brief conversation with Timothy, Lily and Harper walked over to the podium. "You're doing great," Lily said. "And I'm actually learning some things I didn't know."

"That's good," Gianna said, removing her glasses and wiping them with a cloth she kept handy. "So, I'm not boring you?"

"Not at all," Harper said. "The stats you showed

are really fascinating. Who knew that, of the three, trust ranked highest in a relationship?"

"I know, that stat rang out to me, too," Lily said.

"But I can see it," Harper said. "When I lost Cade's trust, everything else didn't seem to matter. He was through with me. Luckily, he gave me a second chance. So I get it."

"Ten minutes is almost up," Lily said, glancing at her watch. "What do you say after this we go out for a quick bite to eat?"

"I'd love to, but what about Rose?" Gianna asked.

"Cade's home with her now," Harper said. "They're having dinner together."

"Okay, then. It's a date. And thanks, girls, for coming tonight. It means a lot."

Gianna breezed through the rest of her presentation, the second half of her seminar smooth and flawless, with no technical difficulties. That was always a plus. She spent some time afterward speaking to students. Some had questions, others simply wanted to thank her for the "brilliant workshop." The compliments gave recognition to her hard work.

She met up with Lily and Harper, and the three of them walked out of the lecture hall together. With the seminar under her belt, she was eager to celebrate with the girls. Maybe have one sole drink of something fruity and delicious. Gage would approve. She could just hear him now, teasing her about it.

Just then, news vans pulled up and men and women with cameras bounded out of them, snapping photos. Gianna had no idea what was happening;

they all seemed to be in such a big rush. She glanced at Lily and Harper and they responded with an unknowing shrug. Baffled, they stood there frozen as the paparazzi swarmed her, sticking microphones in her face, shouting questions at her.

"Professor, what do you have to say about your fiancé cheating on you?"

"Did you know about his affair with Leah Marie?" someone shouted.

"Have you seen the photo of them yet?" another one called out.

Curious students walked up to the unfolding scene, and Gianna and her friends were suddenly surrounded by a sizable crowd.

"Didn't you just give a lecture on relationships, Professor?" a female reporter asked.

The questions came in rapid succession, and Gianna had absolutely no clue what they were talking about. Harper, more astute on paparazzi tactics, pulled up a photo from social media on her phone. "Maybe this is what they're talking about, honey."

The sympathy in Harper's voice had her glancing at the photo, still stunned at the onslaught of questions. There were Gage and famous actress and leading lady Leah Marie in a lusty lip lock, two of the beautiful people coming together like a scene on a movie poster, leaving no room for doubt as to what was going on. Photos didn't lie. Not this one, anyway. It was clear what Gage was doing.

Blood left her face, her body shook and she wasn't sure if she trembled only on the inside or if her shaking was visible to everyone. She didn't much care. A knife sliced her heart in two, the pain and shock almost unbearable. Why had Gage called her last night and then again this morning? To make sure she'd play nice? To keep her appeased…*and satisfied.*

Oh, God.

Lily and Harper stood like soldiers beside her, flanking each side, but even their strength couldn't bolster her. She wanted to sink into the ground, never to appear again.

Why had Gage done this to her?

Why couldn't he have waited until their little charade was over?

Why had he humiliated her this way?

"It could be innocent, Gianna," Harper whispered in her ear. "Stand your ground. Don't assume anything until you speak with Gage."

Lily took her hand. "My brother wouldn't do this. There's got to be an explanation."

The image of Gage kissing Leah Marie wrecked her inside. But she had to answer the probing questions being tossed her way. The reporters would never leave her alone otherwise.

Stick to the plan, her intellect told her. *Don't stray. Wait to speak with Gage.* Harper and Lily encouraged her to do just that.

"What do you have to say, Professor?" Another microphone was shoved in her face. She gritted her teeth. Why anyone would choose to go into a profession where your every move was scrutinized like this was beyond her. It only proved how different she and Gage were.

Gianna stood tall. She mustered her courage, even as the knife twisted inside. "I trust my fiancé," she told them. "Gage is a good man. And you're all making too much out of this."

"So, you don't think he's cheating on you?"

"No, I do not. It's obvious he's at a charity event. Trying to do some good."

"Wasn't your seminar tonight about trust?"

"Partly, yes," she answered, keeping a straight face. "I have faith in Gage," she said, her newfound acting chops on full display. "We trust each other."

Lily and Harper grabbed her by the arms and edged her away from the news reporters. They didn't follow. They'd gotten what they wanted from her: her undying loyalty to Gage. A loyalty she no longer believed in. Once in the car, Lily floored it, getting them away from the vultures who'd love to eat her alive.

The first thing in the morning, Gage's phone rang, waking him from a sweet dream about Gianna. When he picked up, Cade and Lily were on the line, giving him a tongue-lashing about something. It took him a minute to clear his head. "Wait, what?"

"There's a picture on the internet of you kissing Leah Marie, Gage," Lily said. She was fuming. It'd been years since he'd heard that tone in his sister's voice. "It looks bad. Real bad, and now it's all over social media. I just sent you the picture. Take a look. Poor Gianna was ambushed outside her lecture hall last night by the paparazzi. It was awful and she's shaken up, but trouper that she was, she defended you and your engagement."

Crap. It was the last thing he wanted to happen to her. "Okay, all right. I have no clue what's going on. I'm coming right home. And listen, nothing happened with Leah Marie. I'm telling you straight."

"Well, don't tell us. Tell Gianna. She's upset. And that's putting it mildly."

"I'll talk to her. I'll explain."

Gage got on the earliest flight he could, and on the way to the airport, his phone rang off the hook. He received dozens of text messages with inquiries about his "affair" with the famous actress and star of *Sunday in Montana*. Granted, the photo had been taken at a precise photo-op moment, where it appeared more fiery a kiss than it actually had been. Hell, the truth was, it had been a quick one-second peck on the mouth that had gotten blown completely out of proportion.

On his flight home, he read everything he could find on the internet about the incident, but what riled him the most was seeing video of Gianna being tormented by the paparazzi outside her lecture hall. Those bastards harassed her into making a comment. And, true to Gianna's nature, she didn't falter. She defended him with such powerful words that tears filled his eyes. She'd been perfect, said all the right things. But it galled him that she was put into that position.

None of this should've happened. It was fake news at its most despicable, a publicity stunt that someone might've engineered, with stories on the internet and social media predicting doom for the newly engaged couple. His biggest concern was for Gianna, but she wasn't answering his calls.

And once he finally got home, he thought better of knocking on the guesthouse door. Instead, he used his key and entered the place. Gianna sat calmly at the kitchen table, drinking coffee.

It was surreal, the calm that surrounded her. While she looked the picture of serenity, his nerves were jumping jackasses. He couldn't control the trembling inside. He'd given concerts to tens of thousands, and yet this one woman, who refused to look at him, jarred his steely resolve.

He moved closer, breathed in the scent of her, all girly soap and sweet shampoo. Her hair was up in its usual knot; she wore gray sweats and an equally drab tank top, her glasses perched on the bridge of her nose. Yet she was beautiful, a woman who meant something to him.

He took a seat facing her. Finally, she lifted her lids to him. Her sage-green eyes were filled with sorrow. It nearly busted him up inside. "Gianna, none of it is true. You know me. I wouldn't do that to you."

"I don't know if I know you at all, Gage." She said it matter-of-factly. But her eyes betrayed her calm demeanor.

"I don't know who took that picture, but it was completely innocent. Leah is a flirt, and before I knew it, her lips were on mine. But the whole thing lasted no more than a second. I moved away from her, and she teased me about being whipped by my fian-cće." He cleared his throat. "Which I am."

Her brows furrowed.

"I mean, she knows I'm…we're engaged."

"But we're not. It's all fake, Gage. I feel like a total fraud."

"Listen, I hated that you had to go through what you did last night." He reached for her hand, and she pulled it away. Okay, so she was pissed. "Those reporters should've never bothered you. It was really nothing."

"Nothing? I was humiliated in front of my students, Gage. In front of the world. I'd worked so hard… Never mind." She sipped her coffee.

"No, I know how hard you've worked these past few weeks. You've been amazing. You are amazing. And I'm sorry. But honestly, nothing like this is ever going to happen again. I promise."

"You can't promise that, Gage. You're a superstar. You're under a microscope all the time. I said I'd help you and I don't go back on my word, but I'm not going to subject myself to any more humiliation. We're not going to live in this house together anymore."

He laughed, and she turned a sharp eye to him.

"I mean it, Gage. We've been playing house, but that's all ending as of today."

"What do you mean?"

"I mean, I want you to move out. You go back to live in the main house. We only see each other when there's a planned event. I'll bide my time and then we'll break up quietly later in the year."

"No." His heart began to pound hard against his chest. The loss stifled his breathing. She couldn't be serious. "Gianna, you're being unreasonable."

"No, Gage. I'm being logical. It's the only way this is going to work between us."

"I wish you'd stop analyzing everything."

"That's what I do, Gage. That's why you and I don't work. We're complete opposites. We both know how this will end. It's better this way. I'm not going to be your bed buddy anymore."

"My…what?" Was that what she thought? Well, hell. He'd never thought of her that way. Not once.

"You heard me."

"I heard you, but I don't believe it. I, uh, what we had together is something special. I thought you felt the same way. I thought…"

"This is hard for me." Gianna gazed down at the table. "Won't you just go?"

"You're kicking me out of my own house?"

She sucked in a breath and eyed him carefully. "You're right. It is your house. If you don't want to go, then I will. I'll move back to my apartment."

"Hell no. Don't do that. I don't want you to leave."

Gage blinked several times. He couldn't let her go. She needed to be here. He had to see her every day. It dawned on him how important she'd become in his life. But she had him over a barrel. He didn't want what they had to end, but he also didn't want her to leave. She'd put her foot down, and he had to allow her to step all over him. Or else lose her for good.

"I'll go. But before I do, I should thank you for

sticking up for me, for us. It probably wasn't easy, but you held your own with those reporters. You kept your part of the deal. And I'm grateful."

"At least there's that. I'm loyal, like a silly little puppy." Gianna rose from the table and walked out of the kitchen, leaving him sitting there alone.

Good God.

He'd never been in love before, but if this was what it felt like, it sucked.

Gage sat on his bed in the main house, his unpacked suitcase beside him.

His mother stood by the threshold studying him. "You've moved back in?"

He hung his head. "That's what it looks like."

"That kiss made the morning news."

"I didn't kiss Leah. She kissed me. And it was over in a second, Mom. Someone snapped a picture to make it look way worse than it was. I didn't think anything of it until Cade and Lily ripped me a new one this morning."

"So Gianna kicked you out?"

He flinched. "That's one way of putting it."

"You're not used to women standing up for themselves."

"What's that supposed to mean?"

"I have eyes, son. I see how the two of you look at each other. You care for her. You may even love her."

Gage ran his hand through his hair. "I don't know, Mom. I've never been in love before."

His mother walked over and sat down on the edge

of his bed. "You know I think Gianna is special. I made you promise not to hurt her. But I don't think you kept that promise."

"Things just happened, Mom. I'm no saint, but hurting her is the last thing I want to do. So she asked me to leave, and I did."

"If you can honestly be happy letting her go, then do it. And both of you will be better for it. But if you have strong feelings for her, do something about it, Gage. Lily tells me there's a professor at the university who's interested in her."

"There is?" Jealousy ripped straight through him. Thinking of Gianna with another man tore him to shreds. He'd never considered she'd have someone waiting for her after this debacle was over. "Apparently, he was at the seminar. Lily saw him talking to her. It's nothing concrete, and it was just beginning to happen before you stepped in and asked her for the biggest favor of her lifetime."

"She never said."

"She wouldn't. And besides, I think she fell for someone else. Someone worthy of her love."

"Mom, if you're scolding me, you're doing a piss-poor job."

"I only want my children to be happy."

"She's done with me."

His mom shook her head, giving him her I-know-better smile. "I disagree. You've been selfish with her, Gage, but you can fix it. I think she's waiting for you to make a move, to prove to her that you care."

"I can't toss her over my shoulder and drag her away like a caveman."

"No, but you could be her knight in shining armor for a change. Think of all the times she's rescued you."

He nodded. His mother was right. "How do I do that?"

"You're smart enough to figure it out, Gage. I have faith in you."

He pushed his hands through his hair. He was a mess, missing Gianna so badly it physically hurt. His head ached, and his stomach was in knots.

"I'll be going now," she said, standing. "You have some thinking to do."

Gage stared at her retreat and sighed.

What was it with women walking out on him lately?

Gianna sat down at the dinner table with the Tremaines. It was the first time in two days she'd seen Gage, and she was dead set against allowing her heartache to show in front of the rest of his family. She'd already been humiliated enough, and she needed to be here, to show them she was doing fine. She'd managed to find time to spend with Rose during the day when Gage was out of the house. So far, her plan was working. She'd avoided him until tonight.

It only made sense that she should dine with his family. She wasn't going to let what had happened between them destroy her other relationships. She trusted them; they had her back. She'd trusted Gage, too, but look where that had gotten her.

"I'm excited for the wedding," Lily said. "Just another couple of weeks and it'll be here."

"Me, too," Harper said. "I can't wait, but I'm a little frazzled with all the plans. Luckily for us, Gianna has offered to help out."

"That's lovely, dear," Rose said, giving her an approving nod.

"Lily, are you bringing a plus-one? You haven't said so yet," Harper said.

"Me?" Lily asked. "Uh, well, I'm not sure. I might."

"I'm sure Nathan would love to take you," Rose said. "As friends, of course."

Color rose on Lily's face. "Nathan has a girlfriend."

Cade and Gage exchanged glances. Something was up with Nathan, but both men kept their lips sealed tight.

"That's news to me," Harper said. "The last time I spoke with him, he said he wasn't bringing anyone to the wedding."

"I wouldn't ask him, so there's no point in talking about it," Lily said, ending the subject.

Too bad—the wedding was a safe enough topic of discussion. During the meal, Gianna made a point of not looking Gage's way too often, but whenever she did, she was met with brooding blue eyes, locked on her.

Dinner ended at nine, and Gianna took a leisurely stroll, heading back to the guesthouse. It was one of the cooler summer nights and crickets serenaded her as she walked. Rapid footsteps from behind slapped against the paved road.

"Gianna? Wait up."

"Go away, Gage." She kept on walking. Her emotions were all over the place, and speaking to him would only make it worse.

He caught up to her quickly. "I just want to tell you one thing and then I'll leave you alone."

"For heaven's sake." She stopped and turned. His face only inches away, a hint of his cologne wafted to her nose, bringing back lurid memories of being down deep under the covers with him, making love to him. The extra stubble on his cheeks and the unruly way his dark hair flipped up in the back was so doggone appealing. Gage was a walking temptation. She needed space between them, not this close contact. She took a step back. "What is it? I know all about the interview tomorrow morning. I'll be there."

She didn't want to go with him, but ever since that photo showed up on social media, he'd been inundated with offers. And because this one news station, and their morning show, *AM Juliet*, had a reputation for being fair to him, Regan had pushed him into going. Gianna was expected to be by his side, of course. "I appreciate that, but that's not it. It's something else."

"What then? Another public appearance?"

He took her hand in his, his eyes searching hers. "I'm giving a concert at the university. I just got word it's a go. All proceeds will go to Learning and Literacy."

Gianna blinked. She couldn't believe her ears. "What on earth?"

"Regan didn't think it was possible on such short notice, but it's happening this weekend. I called in a ton of favors. The band is donating their time. Tickets are set at ten dollars, so all the students and anyone else who wants to attend will be able to. We'll raise a lot of money for the charity."

Her eyes burned, but she refused to cry. She didn't know what to make of this amazing and generous gesture. "Gage, I...don't know what to say. Wh-why are you doing this?"

"I'm doing it for you, Gianna. Because it means something to you. And so many kids will benefit from this. I only wish I'd thought of it sooner."

"It was your idea? Not Regan's?"

"This one is all on me."

Was he doing this for the positive publicity? She could never be sure. But she found sincerity and the yearning to please her in his eyes, on his expression. It really didn't matter why he was doing it. Her favorite charity would benefit, and she loved the idea of that more than anything else he could've done.

"Gianna, I hope you know how much I care about you."

She nodded, not sure what to believe, but she wasn't going to argue the point.

"Thank you for this. I'm totally surprised and *grateful*." She stood on tiptoes and brushed her lips to his cheek.

A low groan emerged from his throat.

She turned quickly and dashed into the house.

Running away from him.

And her emotions, which were, at best, teetering on the edge.

The next day, Gage entwined their hands as soon as they got out of the car and maintained the contact as they walked into the television station. He wore his black John B. with a fancy tan shirt and string tie. He was the picture of a superstar, his demeanor, his presence confident and commanding. He held her close to him the entire time. When it was time for him to go onstage, he gave her a kiss backstage, a sweet brush of the mouth, and walked onto the set of *AM Juliet*.

During the interview, he was brilliant in his handling of the Leah Marie incident, claiming it wasn't anything but a friendly kiss. A full unedited version of a video surfaced days later showing the truth, the kiss barely lasted a second, shutting down rumors of an affair. But Gage also used that time to announce the charity event happening at the university. He made sure television viewers knew how to get tickets and even offered to hold a meet and greet before the show to raise additional funds. He was smooth, working the audience and the host of the interview. While most people would find that assuring and even admirable, she found his charming nature suspect. He could turn it off and on like a light switch. Which Gage was he? Did she even know?

Their worlds were so different, and yet she'd managed to fall in love with him.

Like so many other wide-eyed women.

Women loved him, men identified with him. He was talented, appealing, gorgeous. But he was also stubborn, set in his ways, annoying and…

Gage spoke her name, and her train of thought shut down abruptly. "Gianna's an amazing woman," he told host Bob Lockhart. "I'm a lucky guy. We hope to be married as soon as our schedules allow it."

Those words stole her breath. If only they were true. Gage was so good at lying. He'd never spoken of the future to her. And why should he? They had a deal. They were breaking up, ending this pretense as soon as his reputation recovered.

Maybe then her life would get back to normal, whatever that was.

After the interview, Gianna and Gage shook some hands before they left the television station. Gage opened the car door for her, and she slid inside, glad the pretense was over.

"I'd like to drive by the university," Gage said. "Scope out the pavilion myself. Is that okay with you?"

"Didn't Regan already do that?"

"She did. She met with the event coordinators, but it's been a while since I've been on that campus. I'd like to check it out myself. Besides, who better to show me around than you?"

She couldn't refuse. He was doing a good deed, despite his motives.

"Okay, but I have to get back by two. I'm helping Harper and Cade with some wedding things."

"Two o'clock? That'll give us some time to stop for lunch. I'm starving."

She huffed out a breath. She didn't want to go to lunch with him. But voicing that would only sound petty. She'd already admitted she was free until two o'clock. "Okay."

They picked up sandwiches at a shop just down the street from the television station and brought the food with them to Fairmont U.

This was home to her. This was where she felt safe and familiar. She couldn't imagine teaching anywhere else. She loved the school and her students. Her mood lightened considerably, and after she gave Gage a tour of the campus, including the building where she taught, Gage brought a blanket out from the car. He laid it down under a cottonwood tree in the outdoor pavilion, and they sat there to eat.

Gianna lifted the sub sandwich to her mouth and took a big bite. Still chewing, she said, "This is delicious."

"Guess I'm not the only one here with an appetite. You're demolishing that thing. And not too gracefully, either."

"You're such a jerk." She punched him in the arm.

He chuckled at her sad attempt to cause injury and grabbed her arm, drawing her close. "But I'm your jerk."

She sobered up immediately. "You're not. You can't be. We're too different."

"What does it matter? So we're different," he said

softly, his hand caressing her cheek. "We have something good, Gia."

He brought his mouth to hers, and her breathing stopped. Her heart pounded in her chest so hard she wondered if the entire campus could hear it. The kiss filled her with warmth and yearning and everything she'd been trying to forget.

Her ringtone stopped her cold. She broke off the kiss and glanced at her cell phone. It was a text message from Timothy Bellamy. He'd been keeping in touch with her on and off for a few months. He'd managed to make it to her seminar and compliment her on it.

"Who is it?" Gage asked abruptly, his beautiful mouth in a frown.

"It's no one. Just a friend."

She put her phone down, ignoring the text. Her lips still burned from Gage's kiss.

"Who?"

"His name is Professor Timothy Bellamy. He's a colleague of mine, if you must know."

A fierce look entered Gage's eyes. "Are you interested in him?" He spoke through gritted teeth.

"After the way we just kissed, how can you ask me that?"

"I can ask. You sent me packing, in case you don't remember."

"He has nothing to do with…us. We are just a charade. We're not real. We never will be."

"Why, Gianna? Why are you resisting so much?"

He pressed her, and maybe, just maybe, telling

him the truth, a truth that had hurt her, would make him understand. "I'm afraid you're like my father," she said quietly.

He blinked a few times. "What does that mean? And be specific."

Gianna spent the next ten minutes explaining to him through tears and stilted speech about her father and the lies her mother had told to protect her and keep her from ever learning the truth. She compared him, maybe unjustly, but she did it just the same, to her philandering father. A man who was full of charm and good looks, a man who seemed to always get his way in life regardless of who got hurt.

Gage listened to her carefully, shaking his head, sympathy in his eyes. "I'm sorry about what you and Tonette went through. I had no idea. But I'm nothing like your father. I'm trying to earn your trust, Gianna."

"To what end? I'm not sure what you want from me, Gage. I'm doing what you asked, helping you get your reputation back. I've lied to a lot of people, and I don't feel good about that. I held my head high and defended you when the Leah Marie photo came out. It was humiliating, but I never let on. That was really hard for me." It hurt to see him with another woman. It hurt to know that their time together would come to an end soon, once he got what he wanted. She hadn't bargained for this. She hadn't expected to fall for him.

"I told you that thing with Leah was innocent," he said. "And I appreciate everything you've done for me. That's why I'm busting my butt to make this concert happen."

"Really? It's not just for the positive publicity?"

His mouth twisted, and that fierce look returned to his eyes. "No, it's not for publicity. It's for you. And you're gonna have to decide whether you believe me or not."

Gage got up and reached for her hand. "Let's go. It's almost two."

Gianna placed her hand in his, but there was no warmth in his touch, no connection. He was cold and angry, and she felt like a heel. She'd told him the truth, and he didn't like it.

She didn't much like it, either.

But her relationship with the truth hadn't changed.

Except now her heart was involved.

And it ached like crazy.

The sound check was done, his band members making sure everything was working and in order at the pavilion. The outdoor stage was flanked on both sides with partitions, and a crew was setting up a pyrotechnic light show to end the evening. Gage liked to give his audience the full treatment.

Cade stood beside him just offstage, and they both watched Gianna, with a pencil behind her ear and a clipboard in her arms, speak to some of the students. She was in her element here, the joy on her face a testament to her true calling.

Gage sighed, his heart heavy.

"Have you told her yet?" Cade asked.

Gage shook his head. "No."

"Because you know what she's going to say?"

"I'm pretty sure of it, Cade. And I'm not sure I'm ready."

"Hell, man. You're getting everything you want."

He'd gotten the news last night that he'd landed the role in *Sunday in Montana*, and now it was just a matter of formalities. Regan wanted to shout it to the world, take out billboard ads, but he'd made her promise to keep it quiet for a few days.

She was here, walking around, making sure the concert would go as planned, even though she was mad as hell at him. He couldn't blame her—she'd worked hard on his behalf, and when they finally got a win in their column, Gage was making her hold back the news.

"I'm not so sure I'm getting what I want, bro," Gage admitted. He was afraid to tell Gianna he'd landed the role. Afraid she'd want to end things early, and he wasn't ready for that or sure if he'd ever be ready for that. Plus, what if Leah wanted more from him than a little harmless flirtation? Maybe taking the job wasn't the best move after all. "Right now, I'm not sure of much."

"Gianna's got you spinning your wheels?"

"She thinks we're not compatible. We want different things in life."

"So then, you're serious about her? Because if you're not—"

"God, Cade. Do I have to hear it from you, too? Mom's already lectured me like I'm a ten-year-old.

I'm not out to hurt Gianna. It's the last thing I want to do."

"Have you told her how you feel?"

Gage ran a hand down his face. "Not in words."

Cade's hand landed on his shoulder. "Buddy, words matter to women. They need reassurances. Hell, we all do. And remember, sometimes it's not what you say but what you don't say that can do real damage."

Gage peered at his brother with newfound respect. How did he get so doggone brilliant? "That's darn good advice."

"I know. Harper taught me well."

Gage laughed.

A few hours later, Gage stood onstage after giving one of his better performances to a crowd of seven thousand fans. He called Gianna up onstage and thanked her for her hard work with the Learning and Literacy Foundation. Taking her hand, he spoke directly to the audience. "We've raised a lot of money tonight, thanks to all of you. And because this is such a special charity, I plan to match the money raised tonight with my own funds."

Gianna gasped, her hands flying up to her mouth, tears welling in her eyes. She mouthed "thank you" and wrapped her arms around his neck. He held on, savoring her warmth, enjoying having her in his arms again.

Immediate applause and cheers broke out. Gage slanted a glance at Regan, who was in the first row. Her face flamed, her eyes piercing his, stone-cold. Usually they discussed everything beforehand, even when he was spending his own money. He didn't make a move without her, but ever since he'd been home this last time, he'd been making more of his own decisions. He smiled Regan's way and shrugged his shoulders. She'd get over it.

He walked Gianna off the stage to stand with the family, front and center. Calls and shouts rang out from the crowd, and he returned to face the audience. His mom, Lily, Cade and Harper were all clamoring for another song, too. He always saved one or two of his biggest hits for the encore.

The crowd quieted as soon as the band started up. He crooned the lyrics to thousands, yet all he could think about was Gianna and her beautiful, stunned surprise when he'd made the donation. Man oh man. He wanted to put that look on her face *for the rest of her life*.

He tripped up on the lyrics, his mind racing a thousand miles an hour, but he made a joke about his "senior moment," and his fans laughed along with him.

A few seconds later, all smiles vanished, and the putrid smell of smoke filled his nostrils.

"Fire!" someone shouted and then more warnings rang out.

He spun around, and flames leaping from backstage surged forward. His band fled the stage, and he jumped off the edge, gathering his family close.

"Let's get out of here," Cade said, ushering Harper, Lily and his mom toward a fire exit.

"Wait!" Gage looked around, panicked, searching the area. "Where's Gia? Mom, where is she?" he shouted over the screams. "She's not here."

"Oh, dear," his mom said. "She said she wanted to speak to you backstage."

Gage sucked in a breath. The stage wasn't fully engulfed yet. "I'm going after her."

"No! Gage!" Regan suddenly appeared, grabbing his arm. "Don't go. You don't love her," Regan shouted with crazy ferocity. "She's not even your real fiancée. Don't risk your life!" Regan broke down, tears forming in her eyes. "Gage, I beg you. Don't go."

"Let go." He yanked his arm free. "I have to find her."

Covering his mouth and nose with a bandanna, he made his way through the smoke and flames. All the while praying for Gianna's safety.

Ten

In her apartment two days later, Gianna balanced her computer screen on her lap and once again viewed the exact moment when her once-stable life had turned to crap. At least a dozen different outlets, including her favorite social media sites, had video of Regan's infamous words revealing to the world that Gianna and country star Gage Tremaine were frauds. The gist was that, as Gianna was giving a lecture on relationships and trust, she was lying and abusing everyone's trust by pretending to be Gage's fiancée. Their hoax had been uncovered. Their lies discovered. Not only had she not saved Gage's reputation, but she'd ruined her own.

"Gianna, would you stop watching those videos," Lily said.

"You're just making yourself feel worse," Brooke added.

Both of her friends were sitting beside her on the sofa, being loyal, being kind, trying to make her forget the scandal she'd helped provoke. "I want to feel worse. I don't want to forget what an idiot I've been. This is a lesson learned times a thousand. I want to keep seeing the fallout, to remind myself that everything was ruined."

"You didn't ruin anything," Lily reprimanded.

"Oh, no? Then why am I sending in my resignation to the university?"

"They didn't ask it of you. You're doing that on your own."

"I have to. I can't face my students. Or the staff. I'm mortified."

"Maybe if you gave it some time," Brooke said. "You love your work, Gianna. It'd be a shame for you to give it all up because of this."

"And why are you trying to make me feel better, Brooke? I've been lying to you for weeks. I hated doing it, not that it makes up for anything."

"I understand why you did it, Gianna. I'm still your friend. Always will be."

Her lips pulled into a frown. Her friends were too good to her.

The sound of Regan's pleading voice rattled through the screen. "You don't love her. She's not even your real fiancée."

"Would you shut that down." Lily reached over and closed the laptop cover. "No more, please. Gage feels terrible about this. He fired Regan. It turns out she was behind some of Gage's scandals. She secretly made trouble so she could fix it and keep a tight rein on him. Keep him beholden to her. She finally admitted she was the one who leaked that photo of Leah Marie and Gage to the press. It's sorta pathetic. She claimed she's been in love with him for years. And it all finally came to a head."

"I know, I read about it," Gianna confessed. "She didn't think Gage would fall for the *mousy bookworm*. Yes, even that's on the internet." Gianna closed her eyes. Her humiliation ran deep, and with each breath she took, her heart ached even more.

"It only proves that not all of it is Gage's fault," Lily said quietly.

"I know that. I promised to do him a favor. It's on me."

"It's not on you," Brooke said, ever her fierce defender. "But, my God, Gianna. He ran into flames to save you. He had no idea how bad the fire was when he ran backstage for you."

"I know. I'll never forget that." She loved him for that. For trying to save her. She would've done the same for him. But it was too late for them. Nothing was right. It was all one big fiasco, and Gianna had given up on the idea of Gage Tremaine.

There was one saving grace—no one had been injured in the fire. While backstage, she'd seen sparks flicker wildly from the pyrotechnic wiring and called 911 immediately. She'd warned everyone behind the scenes to get out, and she'd rushed out, too.

By the time Gage had found her, she was already back with Rose and his family.

She'd never forget the look of relief on his smoke-stained face. It had brought tears to her eyes. He'd grabbed her and hugged her tight, kissing every inch of her face. It was a perfect moment in time, but the before and after would never be perfect, so she'd backed away from Gage.

Letting him go.

Freeing herself, too.

The damage to both their reputations was done.

Their little pretend engagement had gone viral.

Gage tossed back his second shot of whiskey and paced the parlor floor. He was in a mood. Hell, he'd been in a mood for the past week. He'd blown it with Gianna. She wouldn't answer his calls. All he'd gotten from her all week was a text thanking him again for running into the flames to save her. How did she put it? *It was a noble and heroic gesture.*

He didn't feel like a hero. He felt like shit.

She'd left the ranch. Left him.

His chest hurt. While everything else inside him was numb.

"Would you sit down, son? You're making me dizzy."

"Sorry, Mom. I'm not good company. I should go."

"Where? The turmoil you're feeling is only going to follow you."

He nodded. "Things got really messed up, didn't

they?" He sat down on a wing chair and faced his mother.

"Things get messy all the time, but usually there's a way to straighten them out."

He shook his head. "Not this time. Lily says Gianna is resigning her position at the university. You know how much she loves that job." He stared into his empty glass, his gut in a knot.

"I do know that."

"Have you spoken to her?"

"Every day. She's struggling, too, Gage."

"It's all my fault. No wonder she won't answer my calls."

"It's not hopeless, son."

"I don't know, Mom. I was a selfish jerk to her. You said so yourself. When I thought Gianna was in danger, nothing was going to stop me from getting to her. I didn't even think twice about it. But now it's maybe too late."

"So you ran into fire for her. And now you're giving up? That doesn't make sense to me. Does she suddenly mean that little to you?"

"Little? How can you say that? I'm not tooting my own horn, but I did risk my life to save her."

"Exactly. You did. So do it again, son. Do it again."

Gage blinked and weighed his mother's words. She was right, of course. She often was. He hadn't exhausted all possibilities yet.

Gianna was worth saving.

Again.

* * *

"Here, put this on, Gianna," Lily said, handing her a red baseball cap. "But first put your hair up."

"And take off your glasses, for once," Harper said. "Be a big girl and put in your contacts."

"Geesh. I didn't know you two were so bossy."

"Just do it," Lily said. "You can't hide out in your apartment forever."

"It's only been ten days."

"But who's counting?" Harper asked. "Oh, right, you are. And so are we. You need a girls' night out. And we're going to have fun tonight, even if it kills us."

Gianna rolled her eyes. "Yeah, you'll die of boredom with me." She looked in her bedroom mirror and carefully put in her contacts. She blinked a few dozen times. This was crazy.

"Honey, you are anything but boring."

Ha. They were right. Her escapades with Gage had been the source of entertainment for the mud-slinging gossip-monger crowd lately. And they hadn't let up.

Her friends meant well, but they'd soon find out she wasn't in the mood for partying. She wasn't in the mood for much of anything. For the first time in her life, she had no plan, no sense of direction, and no amount of alcohol consumption was going to change that. "All right, I'll go for an hour. But that's all."

Lily exchanged glances with Harper. "An hour? You are too generous, my friend."

"After the first thirty minutes, you won't want

to leave. Trust me. Eddie makes this Texas Tumbler that'll wash all your cares away."

"Okay, but just one. Gage says I'm a liquor lightweight."

Lily smiled. Harper smiled. It was the first time she'd referenced Gage to anyone these past few days.

"One might just be enough," Harper said. "Now, are you ready?"

"I don't know, did you disguise me enough? What's one more scandal anyway, if I'm found out?"

"Hey," Lily said. "We're going to have fun, not take you to a pity party, so knock it off."

Gianna chuckled, nodding. Lil was right. She'd allowed herself a nice long pity party, but it had to end. And tonight was the night. "Okay, I'm ready."

The three of them jumped into Lily's car, and she drove to downtown Juliet, parking in front of Eddie's Bar and Grill. It was in the older section of town, where time had stopped and the shops and establishments paid homage to the past.

Luckily, the place hadn't started jumping yet. It was early, and she was grateful for the lack of customers. They took seats up at the bar, Lily ordering three Texas Tumblers.

The drinks were placed in front of them pretty quickly. Gianna took her first sip, and then another. "This is delicious. What's in it?"

"What isn't in it," Harper said, "is a better question."

Suddenly, Gage's face appeared on the flat-screen television nestled between the liquor shelves behind the bar. He was being interviewed by prime-time national host Lucinda Day.

"I'm leaving," Gianna said, swiveling on the bar stool, ready to get down.

Harper and Lily grabbed her arms, one on each side, stopping her motion.

"Did you set this up?" she asked, feeling their possible betrayal down in her bones.

"I swear I didn't know a thing about it," Lily said earnestly.

"Neither did I," Harper confirmed. "But we're here, and we're not going to run away just because Gage is on TV again."

"Again?"

"Yeah, he's been on a lot of the talk shows this week."

"Why bother?" she asked.

"Maybe we should just listen."

She was trapped. By her friends. By her own curiosity. What on earth did he possibly have to say now?

"Can you turn that up?" Lily asked the bartender.

And then Gage's voice came through loud and clear. "...yeah, my engagement started out as a publicity stunt. But the rest of it is all true. The two of us have been friends for years. Our families were close. And Gianna and I always had...something special."

"Rumor has it, she has a nickname for you," Lucinda said.

He chuckled, his eyes gleaming. "Yeah, she calls me Brickhead." He leaned back in his chair, the picture of confidence. "It's pretty obvious why. She's so intelligent it makes my head spin sometimes."

"What do you call her?"

"Brainiac. Ever since we were kids."

Gianna slumped in her seat. Why, oh why, couldn't Gage let it be?

"The truth is," Gage went on, "I never thought I'd fall for her. We've been family friends for years, but we'd never even liked each other much."

"What changed?" Lucinda asked.

"I got to know her. Really know her. She's amazing. Smart, beautiful, sassy. She was never afraid to tell me no."

"And you liked that?"

"I *loved* that."

Lily squeezed her hand, and Gianna closed her eyes. It hurt to hear him talk about her this way. They were done. D-O-N-E. And there was no getting around it.

"Some say you're only here giving this interview to repair your reputation."

"My reputation will survive. It's Gianna's reputation I'm concerned about. She's worked superhard to get to where she is today. She's dauntless in her pursuit of education. None of this was her doing. It's all on me. I take full responsibility."

"So why come clean now?"

Gage gave her his world-class grin. "Why now? Because I have a newfound relationship with the truth. Gianna taught me that."

Gianna slugged back the rest of her drink.

"Wow," Harper whispered.

"I know, right?" Lily said.

"So what is your truth, Gage Tremaine?" the interviewer asked.

"My truth? That's for Gianna's ears only."

"I think we can guess. We've all seen the footage of you running into flames to save her."

"Yeah, and I'd do it again and again."

"Seems to me, your fans think you're a hero. Maybe you're right. Your reputation will survive all this. We're almost out of time, but there's one more question I need to ask. You're thirty-two years old. And you've never made a commitment to a woman. Have you ever been in love?"

Gage shook his head. "No, never. Not until now."

Not until now? Gianna's heart trembled. "Bartender!"

She needed another drink. She needed sustenance. She needed strength. Of course, her friends would say Gage was telling the truth. But how could she know for sure? How could she ever believe in him again? He'd said he had a newfound relationship with the truth. That line really got to her. "He stands to gain from this interview. By admitting what happened he's getting sympathy and…and…"

"He's telling the truth, Gia. I know my brother," Lily said.

"Cade tells me Gage is crazy about you," Harper added.

The bartender slid another drink her way, and she downed half of it in one huge gulp. "Can we please not talk about Gage anymore? We're supposed to be having fun."

Lily shook her head. "Girl, you might be a brainiac, but, right now, brickhead is a better description of you."

"Fine, fine. Call me whatever you want, just keep the drinks coming."

After his interview with Lucinda Day, which went better than he imagined—and he'd imagined it going pretty badly—he picked up a sandwich at the diner down the street from the television station to eat at home. Usually he'd have dinner with Regan after something like this, but that ship had sailed. Her claims of love didn't persuade him. She'd been sabotaging his relationships and making herself shine in the aftermath, and he'd been too blind to figure it out.

He'd been pretty dense about a few other things, too. And he was doing what he could to remedy them.

His phone rang, and Lily's image appeared on the screen. It was after ten. Usually she didn't call so late. "Hi, sis."

"Gage, thank goodness I got a hold of you."

There was panic in her voice. "Why, what's wrong?"

"God, Gianna's gonna kill me for calling you, but we're at Eddie's in town. We, uh, we took her here for a girls' night out. She didn't want to come, and now she's refusing to leave. She's had quite a bit to drink."

"Crap, Lily. You know she's not a drinker."

"I know that now. We've been trying to get her

to leave. But Harper and I can't very well drag her out of here."

"I'm just down the street a ways. I'm coming. Be there in five."

Gage floored the engine and pulled up at Eddie's, his heart racing. He had no clue what to expect when he entered the bar. It was smoky and dark, the scents of hot wings and fries permeating the room. He found Gianna sitting at the bar, giggling with no one in particular.

Lily spotted him and ran over to him. "Thank goodness you're here."

"How many has she had?" he asked, keeping his eyes on her from behind.

"Four," Lily squeaked.

"Beers?"

"Texas Tumblers."

"Oh, man, Lily. Are you nuts?"

"I know. We just wanted to cheer her up."

"Why don't you and Harper go on home? I've got this."

"You sure? She's not gonna to be happy to see you?"

"That's too bad. She's gonna see me, and I'm not leaving here without her."

"Okay. Thanks." Lily rose on tiptoes and kissed his cheek. "And, bro, don't waste this opportunity with her. Tell her how you feel."

He scowled. "Right now, she doesn't want to know how I feel."

Lily patted his shoulder. "When did you get to be such a freaking hero all of a sudden?"

"Just go, little sis."

After Harper and Lily left, Gage walked over to the long oak bar and sidled up next to Gianna. He leaned his elbow on the bar and faced her. "Hi."

Gianna stopped with her glass halfway to her mouth. Gage took the glass from her hand and set it down. Her lack of reaction said it all. Well, she did blink a few times.

"Wh-what are you d-doing here?"

"I felt like having a drink."

"Have o-one with H-harper and Lily," she said.

"They left."

"Party p-poops." She giggled her head off. Apparently she thought that was funny.

"You know you're gonna be sick tomorrow."

"But th-there's always r-right now." More giggles.

Gage sensed eyes on them. He'd been recognized, and pretty soon everyone in the place would be whispering behind their backs. "We have to go, Gianna. Don't fight me on this, okay?"

"I d-don't want to go r-right now."

"We're leaving. Now, either you come with me, or I pick you up and carry you out of this place. Your decision. Make it quick."

She surprised him by swiveling around immediately. She put her feet on the ground and stood. But the rest of her swayed off-kilter, and he caught her just before she face-planted. "I d-don't feel so g-good."

"Hang on, sweetheart." He picked her up and carried her out of Eddie's.

"Is th-this kidnapping?" she mumbled.

"It kinda is," he said. "You can have me arrested tomorrow."

Gage maneuvered her into his car and buckled her in. By the time he climbed into his seat and turned on the ignition, she was fast asleep. Man, her head was going to feel like lead in the morning. She'd be lucky not to toss her cookies tonight.

He should take her to her apartment, but instead he steered the car toward the Tremaine estate. She belonged there, and he was going to make her see that, one way or another.

At the guesthouse, he tucked Gianna into bed and slid in beside her. She moaned a little bit, holding her stomach. "It's gonna be okay, Gia," he murmured, trying to ease her discomfort. It wrecked him that she was in pain. He'd certainly been there, done that, so he knew the kind of cramping she was having.

After a time, she slipped into a quiet slumber and Gage removed himself from her bed. He hated leaving her, but this had to be her decision. He set a glass of water and two aspirins on the nightstand for her. She'd know what to do with them. Then he took up a spot on the sofa and hoped for the best when morning came.

Gianna woke up in the guesthouse bedroom, the scent of coffee brewing in the kitchen oddly not rattling her too much. She felt at home here, and she barely remembered what had happened last night, other than Gage showing up at the bar. Things were fuzzy after that. Had he picked her up bodily and carried her out of Eddie's? Had he brought her here and tucked her into bed?

She smiled.

He had.

He was here now, attempting not to make noise in the kitchen.

Her head ached, but it would've ached more if she hadn't taken the pills that had magically shown up on her nightstand. And her stomach ached, too, but only a little. She'd endured most of the cramping in the wee hours of the morning.

She moved slowly, putting on a big old gray sweatshirt, setting her glasses on her nose and twisting her mop of hair at the top of her head.

This was who she was in all her comfortable glory. She had to remind Gage of that.

She made her way to the kitchen. Gage was pouring coffee into two cups. She stood at the edge of the room, eyeing him. He was in the same clothes from last night, looking rumpled and gorgeous.

"Tell me something, Gage," she said, and her heart stopped when he looked up, coffeepot in hand. There was a light shining in his eyes, a blue beam of emotion that struck her instantly.

"Anything."

"Don't you believe in roses and candy? Or sweeping a girl off her feet? And I don't mean picking her up bodily and carrying her out of a bar. What kind of guy goes on national television to profess his love? Why, with you, are cameras always rolling?"

"Good morning to you, too, Gianna. How do you feel?"

"Better than I did last night. I guess I got lucky this time."

"Come and have some coffee. It'll be good for you."

"Answer my question, Gage."

He set the coffeepot down and strode over to her, capturing her gaze. Goodness, she could melt right into those intense blue eyes. "You're not the roses and candy kind of girl, sweetheart."

"I'm not?"

"No, you're way more than that. You're the kind of woman that gets into a man's head until he can't think straight."

"I am?"

"The kind of girl whose brains are ultra sexy."

She gulped. "Ultra?"

He nodded.

"I don't even have a plan for my life now, Gage. I'm lost, I don't know what way to go."

"You're not lost. You haven't lost anything. Not your job. Not your friends. Not anything."

"How can you say that?"

Tenderly, he brushed a stray strand of hair away from her face. The sweet caress streamed all the way down to her toes. "I can say that because I've spoken with the president of Fairmont U. He doesn't want your resignation. He never did."

"And how much did that cost you?" she asked, her mind kicking into high gear.

"Not a penny. They love you. They want you to come back. Gianna, after I explained my part in the charade, the president understood everything."

"You mean, I have my job back?"

Gage's grin wiped out all her doubts. "You never lost it, sweetheart. But I do suggest that you take a leave of absence."

"Why?"

"For one, I declined the role in *Sunday in Montana*."

"You did? But that's why we entered into the charade in the first place. For you to get that role."

"I don't need that gig. I'm a musician, not an actor. I can't believe how relieved I feel about that. I don't want to be away from you for three months."

"No?"

"No, can't do that. I'd miss you too much. Besides, we're going to Europe as soon as we can arrange it. I hear Italy and Greece are beautiful this time of year. And I think we can both use some time away."

"You do, do you?"

"Yeah, I do. Fact is, I pretty much have everything I want. That is, *if I have you*."

"Me?"

"Yeah, you, sweet Gianna."

Gage stared her straight in the eyes and then lowered down on one knee and took her hand. "You're beautiful, Gianna, inside and out. I love you. With my whole heart. I've never been in love before, so it took me a long time to recognize it, but I can't imagine my life without you."

"Gage," she whispered. Was this really happening? Her heart filled with joy.

"I want you by my side, always. I want everything with you. A home, a family. I want us to grow old together. I want to take you on that trip to Europe and go to the opera with you. I want all that, but I have only one condition. You go as my wife. Gianna, will you marry me?"

Tears dripped down her cheeks. "Oh, Gage. I love you, too. And yes, I'll marry you."

Gage stood then, and she fell into his arms. He hugged her tight and brought his mouth to hers. The delicious taste of him filled her senses. The kiss was as perfect as the man she was going to marry.

She put her hand on his stubbly cheek, and her heart swelled. "I was wrong about you, Gage. You're nothing like my father. I'm sorry to have compared you to him. Can you forgive me?"

"I do. I will admit, I gave you reason to doubt me. But never intentionally. I guess I am a brickhead sometimes."

She smiled. "You're a good, good man, Gage Tremaine. And I'm never going to hear the end of it from Lily. She's been in your corner the entire time."

He laughed. "That's good to know, sweetheart." He brought his lips to hers again, this time more urgently. This time with a promise of what would come later tonight. She could hardly wait.

"You're my fiancée for real this time," Gage said, stroking her cheek gently.

"And I am yours. We're really engaged now."

"I've never been this happy, Gianna."

"Neither have I, my love."

She smiled. Their future was secure now.

With no cameras rolling.

* * * * *

Don't miss a
single book in
The Texas Tremaines series
by USA TODAY *bestselling author*
Charlene Sands!

Craving a Real Texan
The Fake Engagement Favor

plus
Lily Tremaine's story,
coming soon from
Harlequin Desire.

WE HOPE YOU ENJOYED
THIS BOOK FROM

⊞HARLEQUIN
DESIRE

*Luxury, scandal, desire—welcome to
the lives of the American elite.*

Be transported to the worlds of oil barons, family dynasties,
moguls and celebrities. Get ready for juicy plot twists,
delicious sensuality and intriguing scandal.

6 NEW BOOKS AVAILABLE EVERY MONTH!

#2827 RANCHER'S CHRISTMAS STORM
Gold Valley Vineyards • by Maisey Yates
Things have been tense since rancher Jericho Smith's most recent acquisition—Honey Cooper's family winery. What she thought was her inheritance now belongs to her brother's infuriatingly handsome best friend. But when they're forced together during a snowstorm, there's no escaping the heat between them...

#2828 BIDDING ON A TEXAN
Texas Cattleman's Club: Heir Apparent
by Barbara Dunlop
To save their families' reputations and fortunes, heiress Gina Edmonds and hardworking business owner Rafe Cortez-Williams reluctantly team up for a cowboy bachelor auction. Their time together reveals an undeniable attraction, but old secrets may derail everything they hope to build...

#2829 THE EX UPSTAIRS
Dynasties: The Carey Center • by Maureen Child
A decade ago, Henry Porter spent one hot night with Amanda Carey before parting on bad terms. They're both powerful executives now, and he's intentionally bought property she needs. To find out why, Amanda goes undercover as his new maid, only to be tempted by him again...

#2830 JUST A LITTLE MARRIED
Moonlight Ridge • by Reese Ryan
To claim her inheritance, philanthropist Riley George makes a marriage deal with the celebrity chef catering her gala, Travis Holloway—who's also her ex. Needing the capital for his family's resort, Travis agrees. It's strictly business until renewed sparks and long-held secrets threaten everything...

#2831 A VERY INTIMATE TAKEOVER
Devereaux Inc. • by LaQuette
Once looking to take him down, Trey Devereaux must now band together with rival Jeremiah Benton against an even larger corporate threat. But as tensions grow, so does the fire between them. When secrets come to light, can they save the company *and* their relationship?

#2832 WHAT HAPPENS AT CHRISTMAS...
Clashing Birthrights • by Yvonne Lindsay
As CEO Kristin Richmond recovers from a scandal that rocked her family's business, a new threat forces her to work with attorney Hudson Jones, who just happens to be the ex who left her brokenhearted. But Christmas brings people together...especially when there's chemistry!

HDCNM0921

*Things have been tense since rancher Jericho Smith's
most recent acquisition—Honey Cooper's family winery.
What she thought was her inheritance now belongs
to her brother's ridiculously handsome best friend.
But when they're forced together during a snowstorm,
there's no escaping the heat between them...*

Read on for a sneak peek at
Rancher's Christmas Storm
by New York Times *bestselling author Maisey Yates!*

"Maybe you could stay." Her voice felt scratchy; she
felt scratchy. Her heart was pounding so hard she could
barely hear, and the steam filling up the room seemed to
swallow her voice.

But she could see Jericho's face. She could see the
tightness there. The intensity.

"Honey..."

"No. I just... Maybe this is the time to have a
conversation, actually. The one that we decided to have
later. Because I'm getting warm. I'm very warm."

"Put your robe back on."

"What if I don't want to?"

"Why not?"

"Because I want you. I already admitted to that. Why
do you think I'm so upset? All the time? About all the
women that you bring into the winery, about the fact that

my father gave it to you. About the fact that we're stuck together, but will never actually be together. And that's why I had to leave. I'm not an idiot, Jericho. I know that you and I are never going to… We're not going to fall in love and get married. We can hardly stand to be in the same room as each other.

"But I have wanted you since I understood what that meant. And I don't know what to do about it. Short of running away and having sex with someone else. That was my game plan. My game plan was to go off and have sex with another man. And that got thwarted. You were the one that picked me up. You're the one that I'm stuck here with in the snow. And I'm not going to claim that it's fate. Because I can feel myself twisting every single element of this except for the weather. The blizzard isn't my fault. But I'm making the choice to go ahead and offer…me."

"I…"

"If you're going to reject me, just don't do it horribly."

And then suddenly she found herself being tugged into his arms, the heat from his body more intense than the heat from the sauna, the roughness of his clothes a shock against her skin. And then his mouth crashed down on hers.

Don't miss what happens next in…
Rancher's Christmas Storm
by New York Times *bestselling author Maisey Yates!*

Available October 2021 wherever
Harlequin Desire books and ebooks are sold.

Harlequin.com